"Take off your clothes," Jake ordered her

"I will *not*," Ellie retorted.

He pulled his gun out of its holster and cocked the hammer. "You're not leaving this room until I get back what you stole. Now, do it."

Something shifted in her eyes. Something catlike and unsettling. "All right," she agreed, unbuttoning her denim britches. "But first you have to tell me one thing. Where exactly are we and how do I get back to Deadwood?"

"That's two things."

She smiled slowly. "Fine. One piece of clothing for each answer, then."

"We're on the *Natchez*, a steamer, heading for St. Louis."

She slid her pants down and kicked them out of the way. "That's one."

Jake didn't react. He couldn't. He was too busy staring at what she was—or rather wasn't—wearing.

"What?" She shifted to give him a better view. "You've never seen a thong before?"

Blaze

Dear Reader,

Some books come kicking and screaming into the world; others are simply gifts. *Once a Gambler,* which I'm thrilled to say is my first Harlequin Blaze novel, was a gift. That's because Jake and Ellie were so easy to love, and because my wonderful editor, Kathryn Lye, took a chance on a time-travel story from *me,* a time-travel virgin! Having written both contemporaries and historicals, though, I found merging these two worlds really fun.

A friend once told me of a weird experience he'd had on a boat one night at a local lake. For a few moments before they vanished, he saw an antique flatboat full of men, poling across the foggy lake with long sticks. They appeared to be from the 1800s and my friend believed he'd glimpsed another time.

You can guess that sent my writer's imagination running hog wild. What if time travel *was* possible? And if you found true love in that other world, would destiny allow you to keep it? That's exactly the dilemma in my novel.

If you've already read the prequel to this story, *Once an Outlaw,* by Debbi Rawlins, my friend and plotting partner, then you know you're in for an adventure. So sit back and enjoy the ride!

Happy reading,

Carrie Hudson

Once a Gambler

CARRIE HUDSON

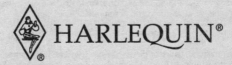

TORONTO • NEW YORK • LONDON
AMSTERDAM • PARIS • SYDNEY • HAMBURG
STOCKHOLM • ATHENS • TOKYO • MILAN • MADRID
PRAGUE • WARSAW • BUDAPEST • AUCKLAND

Recycling programs
for this product may
not exist in your area.

ISBN-13: 978-0-373-79465-2
ISBN-10:   0-373-79465-7

ONCE A GAMBLER

www.eHarlequin.com

Printed in U.S.A.

ABOUT THE AUTHOR

Carrie Hudson lives in Southern California and worked in Hollywood as a successful commercial actress before giving it all up to follow her dream of becoming a writer. Creating stories that spin on an axis of love and happily-ever-after comes naturally for this incurable romantic. It's not entirely her fault. She's married to a fabulous guy, has two wonderful children and a pair of mismatched cats who spend much of the day licking one another, madly in love. Really, what chance did she have? To contact the author, please visit www.carriehudsonbooks.com.

To my dear friend Debbi Rawlins,
who shoved me back up on the horse when
I needed shoving and for loving the whole
Old West world as much as I do.

And as always, to my husband, David,
without whom I could never do this.
You're the best.

Acknowledgment

In 1874 George Armstrong Custer's announcement that gold had been discovered at French Creek triggered the Black Hills Gold Rush and the rise of Deadwood. The town sprang up quickly, reaching a population of over 5,000 in an alarming amount of time, and attracting a slew of businesses from saloons to brothels to dry goods stores. Buildings were hastily erected and sometimes even tents were used by vendors, as well as attorneys plying their trade, but for the purposes of this book, I've focused on a much more scaled-down version of the camp. Also you will note that during this period, some of the newer inventions enjoyed back East were not yet available to the citizens of Deadwood.

1

Question: Is it always fundamental to know one's destination? Or, can not knowing be the path to truly knowing?

(A little-known Confucius-ism)

Hollywood, California
March 2009

THE PHOTOGRAPH of Ellie and her sister swam just beneath the surface of the chemical bath, appearing slowly as if rising through a bank of fog. Like a puzzle it evolved: her own dark hair, their clutched hands, her sister Reese's head thrown back in laughter—until finally the two of them appeared just as Ellie remembered they'd been that day before everything had changed.

That day, she remembered, was a Friday. She had worked for thirty minutes setting up that shot and kept getting it wrong. Either she would miss getting seated altogether before the autoshutter went off, or Reese would make a silly face and they would dissolve into laughter again. There was a decent posed shot—all terribly serious. Even she had to admit they both looked great, but she didn't like it as much as this one. This accidental one. This shot captured the real Reese. Not the physician the world knew on TV news shows. Not the brilliant, accomplished one their parents adored.

But simply her big sister whom she had loved.

She transferred the photo into the stop bath, swirling it beneath the surface with the plastic tongs. She liked the contrast on this one. It was good and she knew it. But that wasn't the point. It wasn't for the show she was putting together. The point was—she'd realized sometime late this afternoon—she'd begun to forget that little dimple in Reese's cheek and the way the lines around her eyes crinkled when she laughed hard. It had taken almost a year to work up the nerve to even develop this roll. Now she wondered why she'd waited so long.

Reese would have said it was because Ellie always did everything the hard way: school, their parents, falling into a career in modeling. "RWC" Reese would call her with a smile. Rebel-without-a-Cause. And deep down, Ellie suspected that maybe her driven, accomplished sister envied that just a little.

She studied the photo under the safelight for anything—any sign that a mere twelve hours after this uproarious laugh, Reese would be gone forever and Ellie would be left alone.

There was nothing. No precognition. No warning. Just two women sharing a rare moment of sisterly hilarity. Maybe that was just how life was. A constant collision of happiness and loss.

"Ellie?" Dane knocked on the makeshift darkroom door. "Are you dressed? It's almost six-thirty."

She looked down at her ripped jeans and fixer-stained T-shirt. "Um…" she hedged, pulling the photo out and slipping it into the third tub containing the rapid fixer.

On the other side of the door, she heard Dane cursing. She couldn't see him, but imagined that about now, he'd be dragging a hand through his perfect dark-brown hair and starting to sweat through the perfect charcoal Prada shirt it had taken him two hours to pick out.

"Just give me a minute, okay? I'm almost done."

"Ah, God, Ellie." The words were gruff, husky, disappointed.

"I know."

"This screening is important to me. You said you'd come, dammit. I need you there."

"I know. I'm coming." She'd done enough red carpets in her lifetime to pave the Great Wall of China, but she detested them. It wasn't that she didn't want to do this for Dane. It was what she knew would come along with it.

"What are you doing in there? Can I come in?"

Ellie switched off the safelight and turned on the regular one. Outside the door the red warning light would no longer be on, and Dane took that as an invitation.

He appeared at the door, looking very Hollywood producerlike in his power suit and spiffy Italian shoes. In another lifetime, Dane Raleigh could have been a movie star, with his looks and his confidence. But now, he was a producer with a film that had made it to screen and that, in this town, was like winning the freakin' lottery.

He glanced down at the photo in the stop bath and

went quiet for a second. Ellie slipped the photo into the hypo fixer.

"So this is about Reese again?"

"Again?"

He slid his hands around her shoulders and turned her toward him. "Just for tonight, can we not put your sister between us?"

"What's that supposed to mean?"

"It means I want all of you tonight. Not fifty percent. Or eighty. I want a hundred percent of you. You know the damned studio has got us opening against *Lands' End,* the best reviewed gangster movie since *The Godfather,* and that behemoth animated kids' movie Pixar Films made about damned ladybugs."

"I know."

"And if we can't get press on this thing tonight, we're screwed for opening weekend. And if opening weekend is screwed—"

"It won't be. And you have me," she said, leaning her cheek against his hard shoulder so she didn't have to lie directly into those rich-colored eyes. "It's just…you know I hate these things. With the paparazzi and the media."

He patted her awkwardly with his palm, distracted by his own problems. "They're just people trying to make a living. And for a girl who spent half her adult life on the world's best runways facing flashbulbs, you should be used to it."

She could explain to him again about the things she didn't want the world to know about her, about how a chunk of her had gone missing after all those years of modeling. She could try to explain that the rock he'd put on her finger a month ago did not give them the right to invade her private life one more time. But she had the sneaking suspicion that Dane liked the attention that came with having her on his arm and the ring making the tabloids. But underneath everything else she believed about him—about them—was the fear that he loved all of that more than he loved her.

He swatted her on the rear and pushed her toward the door. "Go get ready. The driver's here in twenty minutes. Let's not keep him waiting."

THE GAUNTLET set up along Sunset Boulevard beneath the historic archway of the old Cinerama Dome came complete with a red carpet and banks of halogen lights. Beacons of bright light pierced the night sky, as heavy banks of clouds hovered over the Hollywood.

There was a deep crowd just outside the railing, which included fans and paparazzi who hadn't been lucky enough to nail a press pass. The media had already swarmed Ross Neil, the only money star of *Ticking Clock!*, and his little-known female costar up the line. Fans were shouting at them across the railing, hoping for autographs or even eye contact.

Ellie touched the jade necklace at her neck, Grandma Lily's necklace, like a talisman. She hadn't taken it off since Reese vanished. And though it complemented the designer canary-yellow dress she'd worn, she didn't care if it did or not. It made her feel safe to wear it.

She'd spent her life, it seemed, at events like this, tugged around by her parents. Yes, they'd brought her and Reese to their movie openings. The happy family photos would show up on the pages of the latest gossip rag with captions about what great parents they were, and wasn't it fabulous that two big stars could keep it all together the way they did? Until they'd gotten divorced.

For a while, Ellie had cherished these red carpet events as the only way she would have any time with her parents. But that was old water, way under the bridge now.

Ellie gripped Dane's hand tighter as they exited the town car beside Caleigh Nguyen, Dane's publicist. The woman was wearing her official I've-got-everything-under-control look and a lime-green, Rachel Pally kimono dress. For about the count of three, they were anonymous. Unnoticed.

Then...all hell broke loose.

Camera strobes flashed. The crowd swelled in their direction. A tribe of paparazzi and media rushed them.

"Ellie! Ellie Winslow! Look this way! This way, Ellie!"

"You look beautiful tonight, Ellie. Can you show us the ring?"

"Dane, have you two set a date?"

And then the zinger she was bracing herself for: "Any new leads on Reese's disappearance, Ellie?"

As she felt her stomach sink, Dane slipped his hand under her arm and guided her away from the reporter who had asked what all the others hadn't had the nerve to. "Just ignore 'em," he told her under his breath.

"Yeah, this is me," she answered, pasting a smile on her face, "ignoring them."

"Good girl." His hand slid down her hip and patted her there—a photo op missed by no one.

Dane turned to the reporters as strobes flashed. "I'd

like to thank you all for coming. This is a big night for us," he told the crowd. "And my beautiful fiancée, Ellie Winslow, is here to support me. My film *Ticking Clock!* has been a labor of love for us and I hope you all enjoy it and, come opening weekend, you bring your friends. By the way," he added with a wink, "we *have* set the date. But that's our secret right now."

She bit the inside of her cheek. And a pretty good secret it is, she thought, since they were about as close to "setting a date" as they were to jetting to the moon.

Ellie allowed herself to be pulled along under Dane's protective arm as he worked the crowd. She bore the questions with a patented smile as photographers clicked away. Caleigh leaned close to her ear and shouted. "He's doing great, right? Look at him. He's a freakin' press monster."

And she actually meant that in a *good* way. "Hmm," Ellie said by way of reply.

"How are *you* doing?" Caleigh scanned the crowd behind Ellie's head like a shark for chum. "Great dress. Who is it?"

"Um, it's a Chlo—"

"Hey, would you mind if I steal Dane away from you for a sec to talk to Lara Walker from *The Inside Edge?* They wanna do a segment on him and I promised them I'd steer him her way." She wrinkled her perfect little nose. "Thanks, sweetie."

And without further ado, Caleigh removed Ellie's hand from Dane's arm and spirited him away, leaving Ellie momentarily alone. "Sure. Why not?" she mumbled, mostly to herself. Then, head down, she made her way toward the theater entrance, hoping to lose herself in the ladies' room for a little while as Dane did the rounds.

A reporter with a TV tabloid logo on her mike thrust it under Ellie's nose, cutting off her path. "Ellie, when are you going to go back to modeling? I hear *Vogue* is still making you offers, and all the runway designers would love to get you back up there for the Paris season."

Ellie sent her an even smile. "I'm actually done with modeling. Completely done. I'm just a photographer now."

The woman tilted her head like a confused rottweiler. "Does being the daughter of film luminaries like Linea Marks and Brad Winslow make it somehow easier to walk away from a career a million girls would give their right arm for, or is it really because you still feel in some way responsible for your sister's disappearance?" She smiled and thrust the microphone back in her face.

"Ya know, I've got to get inside now." *You slime-sucking codfish.* "Would you excuse me?"

"Word from the South Dakota police," the reporter continued, "is it's a cold case now. Care to comment on the fact that they've given up on finding her?"

"No, I wouldn't." She smiled an evil smile at the bottom-feeder's cameraman and plunged into the crowd, feeling a panic sweat travel up her chest toward her face. She dug into her purse for her cell phone. Elan, Dane's driver, would come and rescue her. Dane would never even know she had gone.

But a tall guy on the other side of the velvet ropes caught her by the arm in the chaos and, with an imploring look, tugged her to a stop. "Please, Miss Winslow. Please just a moment of your time."

Except for the facial hair—the Colonel Mustard goatee and mustache, and the way he was dressed, in an ill-fitting, poorly made windowpane-check suit that looked like it might have been borrowed from an old theater company—he wasn't bad-looking. And the gold watch fob dangling from his front pocket looked...well, real.

Desperation glinted in his world-weary blue eyes. She suspected he wasn't more than thirty, but appeared older. His grip was strong.

"Please," he said, "it's taken me so long to find you."

He wasn't the first crazy fan who'd laid hands on her, and he wouldn't be the last. Ever since the swimsuit issue she'd done for *Sports Illustrated,* they'd crawled from under the oddest rocks to get a closer look at her.

She tried shifting from his unyielding hold and glanced around to see a burly security guard dressed all in black heading her way. "Let go of me now or I swear they'll bodily remove you," she warned.

He did. Instantly. Ellie pivoted to make her escape.

"It's about your sister," he called after her over the din around them.

She exhaled sharply and turned back on him. "When the hell will you people stop—"

"You're almost out of time." His gaze fell to the necklace at her neck.

She narrowed her gaze at him. *"What?"*

"You must look for the photo."

"What *photo?*" Her mind skipped back to the dark-room and the photo she just developed. To the smile on Reese's face.

The refrigerator-shaped security guard with the buzzed haircut was almost on them, barreling toward them as if he'd skipped breakfast.

Urgently the man leaned into her. "You must go back to the beginning. To the trunk. That's how you'll find her."

"Trunk?" Uneasiness frizzled up her spine. "Who are you? And what do you know about my sister?"

"Hands off the celebrities, *amigo.*" The guard shoved himself between them, grabbed the stranger's arm and yanked him practically off his feet. "No touchy, touchy."

Ellie backed up a few more steps, muted by fear.

"Please," the man shouted, trying to be heard above the noise of the shouting fans. "I just need to—"

"Sorry about this, Ms. Winslow," the guard said, as he hauled Colonel Mustard toward the curb. "Man, the *locos* that show up for these things, eh?"

"In two days," the man shouted over the triangle of the guard's arm, "it'll be too late! I beg of you! I won't be able to help you after that!" A moment later he was swallowed by the crowd and disappeared.

Frozen in place, Ellie stood watching the humanity close in around them as if they'd never been there. Gradually, all the shouting disappeared, and the crowd blurred into a hazy halo around her.

Because all she could focus on was an image of that antique, humpbacked trunk in Grandma Lily's attic— the last place she'd seen Reese alive.

"So let me get this straight," Dane said three hours later as she lay sprawled on top of his bed watching him undress. "The crackpot of the century shouts Chicken Little warnings at you at my opening, you actually *fall* for it, and now you're jumping on the next flight to Deadwood?"

"Actually," Ellie commented, rubbing the ache in her temples, "it's not a straight-through flight. It's—"

"God almighty, Ellie." Barefoot, he sauntered closer, working the diamond-studded platinum cuff links out of his sleeves. "Maybe you should be passing out dollar bills to the hopeful drunks down on Los Angeles Street, or…or better yet, buy stock in video recorder technology." Dane tugged off his shirt and tossed it onto the leather club chair near the walk-in closet.

Ellie rolled over and buried her face in the royal-blue down comforter. Dane's scent clung to it and she turned her head. There was no arguing with his logic. Of course he was right. She shouldn't go. But she *was* going. As soon as she got rid of this headache.

"And while we're on the subject of believing, could we just, for one minute, celebrate the fact that the critics freakin' loved my movie tonight? It was a smash. Did you hear the applause at the end? There's even some Oscar buzz already."

She was a terrible person. A terrible, terrible person. "I know," she said. "Congratulations. That's really… wonderful, Dane."

"Thank you," he said, his weight on the mattress tumbling her sideways toward him. He rolled her over and settled himself down on top of her. There was no mistaking what he was after. A little victory dance after his victory. But she wasn't in the mood. In fact, she was having trouble remembering the last time she'd been in the mood for sex with Dane.

Sliding a coppery strand of hair out of her eyes, he kissed her on the cheek. "Hey, I know you miss your sister. But, babe, she's gone."

He said things like that, so offhand that he might as well have been talking about a misplaced parking ticket. Or his ex-wife. It made Ellie wonder sometimes if she was making a mistake. Had she settled? Or was she being too critical?

"And this guy…he's probably a junkie. A wacko. A fan. I'm hiring some personal protection for you."

Ellie's fingers dug into his chest. "Absolutely not," she insisted. The last thing she wanted was some LAPD flunkie shadowing her every move. That was Dane's job.

She frowned. Wait. That didn't sound right.

"Who knows what that lunatic was really after," he said, kissing her jaw.

"He told me the answers were in the trunk. That photos didn't lie. And something about time running out. He said I only have two days."

"Yeah. In two days we'll have that freak in custody." He dropped his mouth onto her neck to explore the pulse throbbing there.

She willed herself to enjoy his kisses. But her mind was elsewhere. "Two days. That's the anniversary."

He sighed. "Who wouldn't know that from just reading the papers?" Intent on his pursuit of her attention, he nibbled at her earlobe.

"But the trunk thing…how would he know—"

He paused long enough to tilt a "C'mon" look at her. "Just a wild stab…but, something that might be in a grandmother's attic…?"

She slid her arms around his neck. Right, she thought. Dane Raleigh, the voice of reason. He was good for her. He was. Who else would put up with the emotional chaos of the past year?

She should just put aside all the doubts about him that had been cropping up lately like bad weeds. He was everything she'd ever wanted all wrapped up in a neat, gorgeous package. He wanted the same things she did: a home, a family—the whole deal. And the fact that he made the most of his engagement to her when he was doing press junkets really shouldn't cancel out all the positives about him. He had good hair, an innate ability to accurately predict the stock market and—

"So," he murmured, adjusting his attention to the plunging vee of her dress, "just try to relax, forget about him."

—and…of course there was something else.

She closed her eyes, willing his mouth to wash all thought of that tall, badly dressed man out of her mind. *Think about Dane's mouth. Think about what his hands are doing to your breasts. Think about—*

"Besides," he added, dragging his palm up her thigh beneath her gown, "I've already called a real estate agent about your grandmother's house. They're gonna auction off what's left inside and sell the place." His mouth paused over hers. "It's already been on the market for a week."

She struggled to push him off her and sat bolt upright. *"What?"*

He rolled to his side, supporting himself on one elbow, looking wary. "Well, yeah. It's time to put all that ugliness behind you, Ellie. Let it go."

"Let it go? Who…who gave you the right to tell me when it's time?" The ache in her temples came rushing back.

"Look, I knew this might upset you, but it's for the best. Linea and I discussed it, and we thought it was a good idea. That place is like an anchor around your neck."

"My *mother?* You went behind my back and— I can*not* believe you. My grandmother left that house in Deadwood to us. To Reese and me."

"Damn, Ellie, calm down. You'll get the money."

She launched herself off the bed and paced to the closet and back. "This isn't about the money. You know I don't need money. And since when are you and Linea so damned chummy? I mean, it's all *I* can do to get a monthly text message from her. And that's usually about how *perfect* you are for me and how she can't *wait* for our upcoming nuptials which, she assures me, she will try her very best to attend, barring any unforeseen movie parts that might interfere." Her voice had risen a shrill two octaves, but she didn't care.

Apparently amused by her outburst, Dane sat down on the corner of the bed and folded his arms across his chest. "We're not chummy. I called her, is all. I thought selling the place would be good for you. For us."

"You did? Really? Well, it's not. It's not good. I hate that you did this without even consulting me." The swell of anger that gathered inside her was like a wave that wouldn't stop rolling toward the shoreline. It had replaced the grief that had pushed her under for months after Reese's mysterious disappearance from Grandma Lily's attic, and it came up at times like this, irrational and a little wild. Talking about Reese as if she were merely an episode in Ellie's past seemed like a betrayal. Assuming the worst about her sister made her furious.

He shrugged his shoulders. "You're not…altogether rational about that house, Ellie. It's just a house. A piece of real estate. It's not going to bring your sister back."

Right. She gathered up her evening bag and the four-inch heels she'd kicked off and hopped on one foot, slipping them back on. "Maybe you're right. Maybe going to Deadwood won't bring her back. But that house is mine and Reese's now. And we get to say when we sell it. And I *am* going tomorrow."

"Ellie—"

"And I'm taking the house off the market."

"C'mon. You're blowing this thing out of all—"

She opened the door and turned back to him. "And you can tell Linea that for me. When you and she have your next little chat, that is."

"Ellie," he called after her, but she was already gone.

2

IT TOOK ELLIE most of the next day to get to Deadwood, with plane changes, car rentals and having to use a detour through the Black Hills for the better part of an hour. When she finally pulled into her grandmother's driveway it was dark. Really dark.

It seemed crazy that South Dakota and Los Angeles shared the same sky. Because this one had a vast, starry splatter of lights arching over it against a velvety black, the likes of which was never seen in California. Too many houses. Too many lights. And even if there weren't, who ever looks up in L.A.?

The cold night air smelled impossibly sweet from the roses that hugged her grandmother's house and from the distant tang of snow sliding down off the jagged mountains. Winter came early here and lasted forever. Hugging herself from the cold, she surrendered to her need for warmth and went inside.

The house smelled musty when she opened it. Ellie flipped on light switches, grateful she hadn't turned the electricity off. It had been months since she'd been here last, and whoever was trying to sell it clearly hadn't been here much, either. There were white cloths covering the furniture and someone had begun gathering things together in the living room, probably for the auctioneer. She triple locked the door and took a deep breath.

With a frown she dragged her suitcase up the stairs toward the bedroom she had always slept in. It was small, with faded striped wallpaper and the twin bed she'd slept on as a girl when they'd come to visit. Made of mahogany with little pinecone finials on top, the bed still bore the signature handmade quilt from their grandmother's hand.

She sat down on the bed and ran her fingers across the patchwork fabric. It was soft and worn with time and love. It smelled like her grandmother in here. She dropped back and rubbed her cheek against the old cotton, feeling tears prick her eyes. As infrequently as they'd managed to see her, Grandma Lily had been a force in her life and Reese's. The only person to see past the photo ops, the trust funds and the Hollywood hype of their lives. Here they were just themselves. Just girls no one knew. Here she and Reese would dream of their futures late at night with the lights out and share secrets they would tell no one else. Here they'd felt loved.

SHE AWOKE THE NEXT MORNING, still wearing the clothes from the night before. Light was pouring in through the undraped window and Ellie sat up, disoriented. God, she'd been exhausted. She didn't even remember falling asleep.

Downstairs she made some coffee in the stove-top antique of a coffeemaker and took a mug with her as she climbed the squeaky stairs to the attic. Swallowing thickly, she opened the door at the top of the stairs and pushed the little button in to turn on the overhead light.

There was a window at the far end, in the eve, and piles of stuff her grandmother had hoarded up here. It was like a yearbook of her life. Little signatures of her friendships and triumphs, and a few of her failures. There was the wide bedstead she'd shared with the grandfather Ellie had never met. He'd died before she was born. There was an old crib and a bassinet, rocking chairs and hat racks. A pair of old wooden crutches and piles of *National Geographic* her grandmother wouldn't part with. But draped across all of these, like spider-webs, was yellow crime-scene tape.

It was this that made the coffee in Ellie's hands shake as she approached the trunk that sat smack in the middle of the chaos. Morning light struck it with a pinpoint ray, as if it were announcing itself as different from the rest. Dust motes swam in the light above it. Ellie knelt down and set her coffee on the floor.

For six months they'd searched for Reese. No stone went unturned, no parolee unquestioned. But in the end, there were simply no clues. No ransom note. No indication according to the police that she had done anything but vanish into thin air.

"You must go back to the beginning," that man had said. *"To the trunk. That's how you'll find her."*

There was no doubt in her mind it was this trunk he meant. This was the last place Reese had been. This was the trunk she'd been exploring when Ellie had run out for coffee, leaving her alone. She'd left the door unlocked behind her. Everyone in Deadwood did. And that was the last time she'd seen her sister alive. She had vanished without a trace.

Ellie opened the lid on the trunk and tilted it back. It appeared to be the same as any of the other dozen weathered trunks piled in the attic. This one, still smudged black with fingerprinting dust, was stamped tin with leather straps and a crinkling wall-papered interior. She began to unload it: there were ribbon-wrapped letter collections and photos and pieces of lace, pressed flowers and hat pins and a velvet crazy quilt that was the most beautiful thing she'd ever seen. Halfway down, she found an antique tintype camera and lifted it out of the trunk.

Sunlight glinted off the large lens as she uncovered it. It was a beauty in mint condition and she couldn't believe they had missed this before. It must be over a hundred and thirty years old. She turned it upside down, examining it from all angles. The initials E.K. were engraved on the underside of it in beautiful scroll lettering. Who was E.K. and how had his camera ended up in her grandmother's trunk? She wondered if it would still work and decided to take it with her when she went back to L.A.

She sat down and placed the camera beside her. She then dug into the trunk again. By the time she'd emptied it, her cell rang. She checked the caller ID and answered the call.

"Okay, are you really back in Deadwood?"

Bridget Meeks's voice made her smile. Bridget, her best friend since high school and unofficial partner in more zany exploits than she could remember, had tracked her down via satellite. Probably in between feedings of her twin baby boys, Lucca and Isaac.

"Yeah," Ellie said. "Nuts, huh?"

"Dane called me this morning as I was wiping the oatmeal off my face, whining about it." She sighed. "He said you two had a fight."

Why Dane felt that he needed to go to her best friend when things were going wrong, she couldn't guess. "That's right. News at six…"

"Everything okay with you two? I mean besides the fact that you're there and he's here?"

Were things okay? She didn't think so anymore. "Do you think I made a mistake, Bridge?" Ellie picked up an old book of historical photography and opened it.

"What? Going to Deadwood?"

"No, agreeing to marry him." That thought hadn't fully coalesced until just now.

An I-don't-want-to-say-what-I-really-think hesitation ensued. "It's how you feel that matters, El."

Good answer. How did she feel? Right now confusion was the only emotion she could pinpoint. It swirled inside her like the dust in the sunlight spilling across the pages of the old book in her hands. "I don't know," she murmured, "maybe I'm expecting too much."

"Maybe," Bridget suggested gently, "it's time you expected *something* of somebody other than yourself."

And there it was. Except for Reese, she wasn't sure she had ever been able to trust anyone. Not Dane, not even his feelings for her. She thumbed through the old book of photographs. Photos of people who had lived more than a hundred years ago stared back at her from the porches of schoolhouses and walkways.

"Do you love him?"

She thought she did. But if this was it—this feeling like there was something big she was missing, could it be the real thing? "Maybe I wouldn't know it if I saw it."

"Oh, I think you would. Maybe you just haven't seen it yet." In the background, Bridget's babies started howling. "Hear that sound? Now that's true love." She laughed like she always did, taking the edge off the seriousness of what she was trying to say. "I'd better go before there's a riot in my kitchen. We'll talk when you get back. Okay?"

"Okay, hon. Thanks. I'll be back tomorrow or day after." They hung up. Ellie tucked the phone in her back pocket and stared at the book in her hands, suddenly wishing she could make sense of this whole trip to Deadwood. That man's words had sent her running here. But was she running toward something or away from it?

She flipped the pages absently until she came across a loose tintype photo tucked into the book of a couple standing in front of an arbor, gazing into each other's eyes. He was tall and good-looking—for the 1800s. Now, if that wasn't love, she thought...

But the pose seemed so unusual for a photo in a time when people had to freeze for minutes to get a good shot. And there was something about it...something about the woman in the picture... It was grainy and faded, but she could swear it sort of resembled... In fact, it looked almost exactly like—

Oh, my God! Like Reese!

Ellie blinked hard, rubbed her eyes, but the woman still looked like Reese. Clutching the photo tighter, she wondered if it was some great-great-relative who had merely looked just like her. But no. There was Reese's dimple, the little mole on her neck. Even her hands… If it wasn't Reese, it was her exact double. But how could someone so long ago look exactly like someone from now?

And then without so much as a warning, the woman in the photo swiveled her head—

—and looked directly at Ellie!

Ellie shrieked and accidentally kicked the camera sitting beside her in her scramble to get up.

As she did, there flashed a brilliant white light. It consumed the air in her grandmother's attic and she felt herself tumbling, falling, as the ground disappeared beneath her.

Until there was nothing at all around her but the white, white light that finally faded into blackness.

ELLIE OPENED HER EYES slowly, feeling muzzy and a little nauseous, as if she'd downed several too many Long Island Iced Teas…and mixed them with a few glasses of Bordeaux. But she hadn't been drinking. Had she? She was having trouble remembering.

A pitchy dark surrounded her, broken only by a hint of moonlight spilling through some kind of slatted wood louvers inches beyond her nose. Even worse, she was flat on her back with her feet in the air, scrunched in some small, cramped place. Something was jammed painfully into her back and she shifted against it.

It felt like…*footwear?*

None of that made any sense. She backed up mentally, trying again. Okay, a second ago, she'd been in her grandmother's attic, then...then *what? Think, Ellie. Think.*

A flash of light echoed in her memory and a feeling that she was falling. Had she been knocked out? Electrocuted? *Died?* Had she gone toward the light?

She lifted her hand to her face and felt around. *Okay...okay. That feels right. Solid. So...good. Alive.*

She felt around the confines of her space. Some kind of a box? Her senses returned to her one at a time: the smell of old wood and musty leather and another smell—like that sharp tang of ozone in the air following a storm; the low rumbling sound of her neighbor's Harley engine idling in the driveway below her grandmother's attic.

She frowned. Wait, not a motorcycle. It was too rhythmic. Too...human.

She clapped a hand over her mouth. Someone on the other side of those slats was *snoring*.

From that deep, dark part of her—that part that had always, since her sister's disappearance, been waiting for the other shoe to drop, waiting for that same brush of darkness to sweep over her, as well—came the awful rush of terror she had known would find her. Whoever had taken Reese had come back for her! And stuffed her in this...this box!

Oh, God, why the hell hadn't she listened to Dane and stayed safely in L.A.? But why couldn't she remember being taken? She had absolutely no memory after going through that trunk looking at old photographs of—

That photo of Reese. In her mind, she watched the woman in the picture swivel a look at her. Maybe she was crazy! Maybe she'd finally lost it. Because that made absolutely no sense. None. Photos do not animate.

Now, an odd calmness filtered through her, spreading a tingling rush of knowledge to the tips of her fingers. Of course. *Of course!*

She was dreaming. This was all a dream. A lame dream. And now, she was dreaming she was in this box. Dreaming there was a man on the other side of this door, snoring.

Of course! All she had to do was wake up.

In the room beyond the louvers, a shadow moved. She shifted her head sideways to get a better look. A woman standing in front of a small, round window lifted a piece of clothing off a chair and rifled through its pockets. Something shiny glinted in her hand for a moment before she pocketed it.

What Ellie did next was totally uncalled-for and—truth be told—unintentional.

Bracing herself, she pressed her hand against the wood slats and pushed. In the next instant, she tumbled ungracefully out onto floor to the sound of the pickpocket's gasp of surprise.

"Hey!" Ellie shouted, but the woman dropped the piece of clothing and, silent as a bat, flitted out the door.

As she quickly struggled to untangle her legs from the stuff in the box, she heard what sounded like a cocking gun.

"Get up," ordered a deep male voice from close by. "Slowly. Don't make me shoot you."

"Whoa, whoa! There's no shooting in dreams," she told him, throwing her hands up in surrender.

"Get up," he repeated darkly, motioning with the tip of that cannon in his hand toward the tall piece of furniture out of which she'd tumbled.

It was prudent to oblige, she decided, and she got to her feet slowly with her hands spread wide. "Okay, fine. But don't point that thing at me."

With his gun still on her, he removed a glass hurricane cover from an old-fashioned kerosene lamp beside the bed, struck a match and lit it. A thin, watery light spilled from the lamp, washing the walls in soft gold.

Ellie's eyes widened. Except for the gun in his hand, and the sheet he was clutching in front of him, he was naked as the day he was born. Against her will and good sense, she stared at him. All of him. He returned the favor, his unfriendly gaze sweeping down the length of her slowly and back up.

He was tall and strongly built. The lean musculature of his chest and arms born of a life lived hard. He seemed tightly strung as if, given provocation, he could just go off like that gun he was holding.

The gaslight carved his arrogance with shadows and fatigue. He wasn't pretty the way so many Hollywood men were. His face had a ruggedness to it, accentuated by the scar that ran along his jawline. His mouth was wide and turned up a little at the corners without trying, but even that perpetual half smile of friendliness couldn't mitigate the bruised look in his eyes.

"What the hell are you doing in my cabin?"

That voice. It sent a shiver down her. "Fair question.

But on the subject of who's supposed to be where," she pointed out, "what are *you* doing in my dream?"

"Your *what?*"

She pointed to his clothing strewn across the floor. "Oh, and you'd better check your things. That little underdressed petunia who was in here a minute ago? She was rifling through them."

He looked confused. What *petunia?* "The only one I see in this room is you." He narrowed a look at her, then glanced around at his clothes. "You think I can't spot a panel thief when I see one?"

"Panel what?"

"Hand it over."

"Hand *what* over?"

"The money. And whatever else you took."

Ellie was outraged. "Whatever *I* took? You've been robbed, pal, but it wasn't by me. And—as if I owe you *anything* considering that minibazooka you have pointed my way—I believe it was a watch she took. Out of your coat pocket."

Some of the color drained from his face. Keeping his gun trained on her, he shuffled to the other side of the bed to pick up his jacket, exposing—she had to admit—a very nice-looking behind.

One-handed, he went through the pockets until he came up with a little leather pouch filled with what sounded like coins. Next he reached under the mattress and recovered a small leather satchel chock-full of what seemed like play money. Relief flickered briefly over his face, but he kept searching nonetheless.

"Like I said, the watch went that way," Ellie reminded him, pointing at the doorway and the now-vanished pickpocket.

He held out his hand.

She pursed her lips. "Don't have it."

A slow, wicked smile crossed his face. "Well, then, you leave me no choice. I'll just have to search you."

3

"OH, I THINK NOT." Folding her arms, Ellie knew she'd sounded a whole lot more certain than she felt.

He wrapped the sheet low around his hips and tucked in the edge as he moved closer, eyeing her jeans suspiciously. "For a woman who dresses in miner's britches and breaks into strange men's berths in the middle of the night, and makes up stories about phantom thieves, your sudden concern with propriety, madam, is ill timed. Put your hands up."

Ellie scowled at him. "Well, you have one thing right. You *are* a strange man. But I still didn't take your watch. Feel free to search me, though. I have nothing to hide. Besides, this is my dream. And…well," she admitted, raising her hands, "you're not exactly trollish."

He didn't spend long trying to puzzle that word out, but shimmied closer in his sheet and nudged her arms up in the air with the end of his pistol. "I suggest you hold very still. I'm surprisingly good with this gun."

"Sure, sure. Nobody really gets shot in dreams."

He muttered something to himself about nightmares, then, he touched her. A slow, one-handed slide down the length of her rib cage, past her hip and around her back.

She inhaled sharply.

From the tips of his fingers to the center of her being, something akin to an electrical charge zipped through her body.

Which was strange because he seemed immune, more intent on what she might be concealing beneath her jersey top. When his fingers reached the clasp on her bra, they stopped and explored for a moment.

"What's this?" he asked, fingering the hooks and eyes.

"Not a watch," she explained.

A droll smile quirked his mouth as he followed the outline of her bra around her rib cage, finding the underwire that ran up the side of her breast. His palm fell naturally against the soft cup and lingered there, testing the weight of her breast in his hand.

His gaze lifted to hers. A bead of sweat had broken out in that little cleft between his nose and upper lip. *Hmm. Perhaps not so immune, after all.* The steely cold barrel of his gun rested warningly against her throat. "Who are you?"

"You first."

"Apparently, you already have the advantage. It was you who broke into my cabin, remember?" The tip of his gun traversed her chest and rested against her belly.

Ellie was too distracted by what the other hand was doing to mind much. "I didn't break in." She leaned close and whispered, "I'm not even really here."

That elicited another grudging smile. "Oh," he said, sliding a palm down the front of her leg, "you're here. You just don't belong here."

She gave him a solemn nod. "Exactly. That's what I've been trying to tell you."

What had she been thinking to agree to this? Even in a dream. His touch was not rough or even angry. It was a slow perusal. A lazy exploration of a foreign object. It was as if he had never touched a woman before. But the expertness of his exploration made it clear that couldn't be true. He rubbed the jersey fabric of her top between his fingers, frowning at it. Then he moved lower, his hand making the trip over her hip bone and down the back pockets of her jeans.

His search missed nothing. Not the square shape of the credit card she'd left in her back pocket, which he glanced at curiously, front and back, before asking, "Your name is Visa?" She replied with a snort. Nor the topstitched seam that ran up the inside of her thigh, which he explored with thorough fascination.

Ellie held her breath. She'd had some vivid dreams before but this one had them all beat, hands down. Her breath quickened and she held herself rigidly, eyeing his weapon. His touch triggered a wick of tiny explosions of pleasure under her skin—and completely against her will, she found herself beginning to sweat. Had Dane ever deliberately touched her this way? Ever taken more than a second to really look at her? She couldn't remember now.

"I will admit," he murmured, scanning the hem near her ankle with his fingertips, "you'd be hard-pressed to hide a toothpick under these."

"You," she began, clearing the frog from her throat, "act like you've never seen a pair of skinny True Religions before."

That disconcerted frown appeared again. "I never talk of religion when I have my hands on a woman, skinny or not," he replied, examining the tiny buckle on her strappy sandal. "And these are...shoes?"

"Very funny."

He straightened, and with his face only inches from hers, she wondered suddenly, and with a hopeful perversity, if he was going to kiss her.

It was her fantasy, after all.

His eyes were fixed on her. Hazel, but for the solitary spot of clear, emerald green in the iris of his left eye. The fringe of lashes—dark and unfairly long—hemmed in the heat of his look. She would have to remember this dream and those eyes for the next time she—

A knock on the door rudely halted the fantasy. Without taking his gaze off her, he spoke to the intruder. "Yeah?"

The door opened and a shorter, pug-faced man poked his head into the room. "You told me to wake you, Jake. It's—" He got an eyeful of her and of the sheet-wrapped Jake and faltered. "Uh, it's time."

"Jake?" Ellie repeated. "That's your name?"

The man at the door slid a look down her, then winked at him. "I'll give you this, my friend. You are good at what you do."

Jake scowled back at him. "It's not— She's not—"

Ellie cocked her head, awaiting his explanation.

"Give me a minute," Jake told him, watching her the way her old cat, Toby, used to watch the lizards he cornered in the garden—like he wanted to eat them. The other man withdrew, leaving them alone again.

"Time?" she asked. "Time for what?"

"The game."

"Ohhh, right…" She nodded knowingly, although it made no sense at all. Any of it. *The game*. Well, listen, babe, I'd better be going. So…just go ahead and pinch me, please."

That earned her another scowl. "What?"

"Pinch me and we'll call it a day. I'll wake up, and…"

JAKE SHOOK HIS HEAD. He'd seen it before. This sort of delusional female. Once he'd known a girl who worked for Tom Blaine at the Rialto in Missouri who carried a little doll around with her pretending it was her baby. This one wasn't too far off that mark, he suspected. But he doubted tonight was her idea. He meant to get to the bottom of it.

"You're one of Hennessy's girls, right?"

"Who?"

"Calder's?"

"What?"

"Did they pay you to roll me? Steal my money? Miss the game?" He moved his hand back up to her rear end and gave her a generous squeeze.

A high-pitched squeak escaped her.

"Awake yet?"

She frowned, looking confused. "I don't think so."

"Take a seat." He pointed at his bed with his gun as he began pulling on the long johns. "Turn your head."

She obliged promptly, but he kept his eye on her. She was the tallest woman he'd ever seen. Those gray eyes were nearly even with his own, and those legs went on and on. The denim trousers didn't fit like any miner's denim, either. They fit her as if she was hot butter and they were the mold. The memory of running his hand up the inside of them made him miss the leg of his pants as he tried to pull them on.

Easy, he thought, trying again.

But it wasn't just her legs. She had a face that could cause a man to throw away a winning hand at faro just to get a better look. And hair the deep auburn color of a banked fire. What the hell was someone like her doing with a bastard like Calder? In his experience, her kind of beauty meant only one thing: trouble. If Calder wants an edge, Jake thought, I'll give him an edge. One he can step right off from.

He pulled on his shirt, watching the way she ran her hand over the bare ticking of his unmade bed like she'd never felt anything like it before. Staring at his whole room, in fact, as if it was a sideshow in a traveling circus, something unreal and beyond her capacity to understand.

Why me? he wondered, fingering the buttons on his shirt. Of all the times for an interruption like her, why now? Just as he was about to win the biggest pot of his life? Well, it was no mystery if Calder was involved. He'd been out to sabotage him since he'd lost his home in New Orleans to Jake two years ago. But to take his watch. That was low.

The deep, harmonic whistle of the *Natchez* sounded, making her jump. Her eyes—Jesus, those eyes—jerked back to him.

"What was that?" she demanded, sounding genuine.

But how could she not recognize the whistle of the very boat she was on?

Okay, he'd play along. "Just the *Natchez* announcing itself around the bend in the river. Or maybe pulling into shore to throw off pickpockets."

Agitated, she stood and ran her hands over the table beside his bed, then handled the brass rail of his headboard.

Then, she squeezed her eyes shut tight. Hard. Then opened them.

Jake's hands stilled on the buttons of his shirt. *What the hell?*

She stomped up and down. Twice. Which only seemed to intensify her agitation. Then, like a lunatic, she reached for the cup of water by the bed and tossed it in her face. Whatever it was she was expecting to happen, didn't, so she wiped the streaming moisture from her nose and whispered, "Oh, my God."

He was staring at her now, half-dressed and dumbstruck.

"What the hell is going on here?" she asked. "I…I can't wake up! I mean if I was dreaming, could I do this?" She dropped the china cup on the floor and it shattered against the worn wood.

"Hey!"

"Or…or this?" Lifting the hurricane glass off the lamp, she dipped her finger into the flame and held it there. *"Ow!"* she shrieked, pumping her hand in front of her, then blowing on her index finger.

"Easy." He stepped in then, grabbing her arms and tugging her over to the bed. Forcing her down, he looked her in the eye, feeling like a man who'd found himself suddenly stranded in the middle of a wide, muddy river. "Listen, Visa," he said, "I don't know what you're doing here, or who put you up to it, but panel thief or not, they should be hung for taking advantage of a deranged woman—"

She held up her injured finger. "See? It actually burned my— *Deranged?*"

But what his eyes landed on instead was the rock on her finger. It was yellow and perfect and didn't look like any paste jewel he'd ever seen in his life. If someone put him up against a wall, he would swear it was a diamond. What was a little pickpocket like her doing with a rock like that? Against his better judgment, he began to calculate what a ring like that might be worth.

He ran a disconcerted hand over his mouth, then bent to pull on a polished pair of boots. "And on that account, I might be persuaded not to press charges."

"Press charges? For what?"

"Breaking into my room." He fitted a pair of cuff links into his cuffs. "Stealing my watch." He tried to avoid looking at the ring, but the sparkle drew his eyes to it again.

"Listen, mister, I did not come here willingly. When I woke up this morning I was minding my own business. It was like any other day in Deadwood."

His hands went still on the buttons of the burgundy silk vest he'd just slipped on. "Deadwood?"

"That's right, Deadwood, South Dakota—"

"You mean the Dakota Territory."

"No, I mean South Dakota, the state."

He chuckled and finished buttoning his vest. "There's no state called South Dakota. The gold rush that madman, Custer, set off two years ago is the only organized civilization in the Black Hills, be that what it is. If you don't count the starving Sioux and Cheyenne up there."

"Custer? As in Custer's-last-stand Custer?"

Jake frowned. "Last stand? That'll be the day someone gets that black-hearted bastard."

She swallowed hard. "I'm gonna hate myself for asking this, but…what's the date?"

"May tenth."

"And the…year?"

"Same as it's been since January first, Visa—1876."

She gasped. "First of all, *huh?* And second of all, *what?*"

He shook his head, slipping on his black coat and tucking the money envelope into his inside pocket. "How long have you been like this?"

"Five minutes. Maybe six. I mean, please, do I look like I'm from 1876?" She spread her arms wide. "C'mon. *Sports Illustrated?* Last year's Swimsuit Issue? You'd have to have been living in a cave to have missed it—" she stopped at his blank stare "—or…or in 1876…"

He raised a brow patiently.

Tears sprang to her eyes. "Oh, no."

He shoved his gun into his gun belt and strapped it on. And from underneath the pillow he pulled a much smaller, palm-size handgun, which he then concealed inside his boot. "I don't have all night," he said at last and held out his hand to her.

"Okay, first, my name's not Visa. It's Ellie."

"Where's the watch?"

"And that little square thing? That's a credit card. Plastic."

"I don't care if your name is—"

"Have you ever seen plastic before?" she asked, wiping her eyes with the heel of her hand. "It's money in the real world. Not that play stuff you have in your pouch. But *real* money. With magnetic strips, computerized chips with security encoding…and…and automatic transfer."

He blinked at her, unsure how to proceed with someone as unstable as she.

"Lady, I don't know what the hell you're talking about." Snatching up the square card from where it lay on the floor, he confronted her with it. "But real money is in that poker game down the hall. A thirty-thousand-dollar pot just waiting for me to claim it. Real money is what I need to get the hell out of here. This… little…bendable piece of…glass—"

"Plastic—"

"—only proves my point about you." He flung the card across the room, where it smacked against the wardrobe. "You're a liar and a thief. And you're— pardon me for saying so—unstrung."

"I'm," she began, looking lost, "somebody in 2009. You may not know that, but I am. I'm on *Vogue* covers."

"*Vogue* covers?" he repeated, unbuttoning his pants and tucking his shirt into them. "What's that?"

Her face clouded up. "You're right. How pathetic is that? The one thing I swore never to trade on, my celebrity, and first mess comes along, what do I do?" She sighed. "Forget what I said. If you could just please tell me how to get back to—"

"Take off your clothes, Visa."

"What?"

"Your clothes. Take them off."

"I will *not*."

"Or," he suggested, "I can just take them and toss you from my room bare-ass naked. On the other hand, I can lock you in here until I get back. Without your clothes, of course."

"You wouldn't."

He pulled his gun out of its holster again and cocked the hammer. "Oh, yes. I would. And you're not leaving this room until I get back what you stole." He flicked the tip of his gun in her direction. "Do it."

Something shifted in her eyes. Something catlike and unsettling. "All right," she said, unbuttoning the top button on her denim britches. "But first you have to tell me one thing. Where exactly are we and how do I get back to Deadwood?"

"That's two things."

She smiled slowly. "Fine. I'll give you one piece of clothing for each answer then."

Why was it that women like her could turn a civil conversation around on a man?

"All right." He cleared his throat. "We're on the *Natchez,* a Mississippi River steamer out of New Orleans heading to St. Louis. We're twelve hours out of Memphis, a day or so more out of St. Louis."

"St. Louis?" she said, talking to herself. "I've flown through there a few times, but only diverting from

O'Hare." She looked up at him. "That's smack-dab in the middle of the country, isn't it?"

He tipped the gun toward her trousers, waiting.

"Oh, right." She slid them over her hips, stepped out of them and kicked them his way. "That's one."

Jake didn't reach for the pants. He couldn't. Because he was too busy staring at her smooth, mile-long legs and what she was—or rather *wasn't*—wearing. "What's that?" he asked, gulping.

"What? This?" She shifted her hip to give him a better view. "You've never seen a thong before?"

He felt color rise high in his cheeks.

"And Deadwood?" she asked.

"Huh—wha—?"

"Where is it?"

"Oh." He dragged his gaze up to hers. "North. About eight-hundred and fifty miles as the fish swims. It's partly reachable by steamer, but this one only works the Mississippi. You'd have to catch one in St. Louis going up the Missouri."

"Interesting."

He gulped again as she tugged off her top and tossed it to the floor at his feet until she was standing before him in some little smooth scrap of fabric covering her breasts that seemed to push them up like a pair of—

"Thank you...*Jake*. How long will you be gone?" She cocked her hip slightly and put her hand on it.

"What?" He was back to looking where he shouldn't.

"Playing your game. How long will it take you to finish?"

"I—" He remembered the gun in his hand and uncocked it. "As fast as I can," he replied.

"Good." She kicked off her shoes and hopped into his bed and pulled the blanket around her. "See you when you get back, then."

He didn't move for a full ten seconds because his feet felt rooted to the floor. She tucked the blankets around her fists and pulled them to her mouth to hide what he supposed was a grin of triumph.

Damn that woman! he thought, gathering up her discarded shoes and clothes, still warm from her skin. Damn the self-imposed celibacy he'd endured for the past three months which now appeared to be near an end. And finally, damn Calder or Hennessy for sending her here to confuse him right before the game.

That was their intent all along, no doubt. Well, we'll see who wins this round, my friends. He turned and walked out the door. And just for emphasis, he slammed it behind him. It reverberated satisfyingly in its frame before he found his key and locked her in.

4

ELLIE SANK BACK on the pillow, her smile slowly fading. *1876?* What the hell was going on? What he'd said couldn't be true. None of this could. And yet…

She threw the sheets aside and tiptoed toward the porthole window. Outside, only a thin sliver of moonlight illuminated the blackness. She squinted into the murky darkness over the ship's bow. Moonlight wavered across the surface of the water like a snake, but did little to reveal the shape of the land on the distant shoreline or, from this vantage point, anything else.

Her mind spun back to the expression on her captor's face as he'd watched her undress. Shocked. That was the word. She'd shocked his nineteenth-century sensibilities. But she'd gotten what she wanted. It wasn't as if she hadn't stripped practically naked in front of strange men before. She'd done it a thousand times backstage at runway shows or fittings. But most of those men had fortunately been more interested in each other than in her.

Jake definitely did not come close to fitting into that category. And beneath the shock, behind those extraordinary hazel eyes, rumbled an unchecked hunger that nearly filled the room. It had scared her. And she didn't want to wait around for him to come back to find out what else he had in store for her. She studied the porthole window beside the bed with a fresh eye and considered her options.

She hurried to the wardrobe from which she'd escaped only minutes ago. If he thought he could keep her prisoner here by taking her clothes, she had a thing or two to teach him about modern women. She had to get out of here and get her bearings. And she had to find a way off this boat.

She pulled his only other shirt off a hook in the closet and tried it on. It would do. His second pair of pants that lay neatly folded on a shelf fit her nearly perfectly. Thank God for tall men. His clothes carried his scent, and almost against her will, she found herself pressing his sleeve to her nose.

Okay, just because the man smells good does not make him a good guy. Who knew what he was capable of?

Something caught her eye, wedged under a saddlebag, and she reached for it. It was the picture. The one of Reese. She must have dropped it in the wardrobe when she'd…when *whatever* had happened to her happened.

She clutched the photo between her fingers, staring at it. If there had been any doubt in her mind before, in the attic, there was none now. It was absolutely her sister, staring at her out of the antique tintype frame. Reese, who had swiveled in her direction with a look that implored her to—what? Help her? See her? Save her? Had this same thing happened to her, too?

But what did that mean? And where the hell was she?

Ellie shook her head and tucked the tintype in the waistband of Jake's pants and decided to think about it later. Right now she had more important things to deal with.

It took some concerted effort to wedge herself through the tiny round window, but she did it, tumbling out onto the deck a few feet below like a landed trout. The pain of the ensuing thump subsided only as she stood up and took in her surroundings.

The place seemed deserted. It was, after all, she guessed from the rise of the three-quarters moon, the middle of the night. Strange time for a card game, but who was she to question the sanity of anything at this point.

Ellie took a few steps to the wooden railing and gripped it with both hands. From the darkness below came the chug of the ship moving through the water and the heavy turn of a paddlewheel slicing through the current. Now she could make out more of the shoreline. It was merely an inky shadow in the darkness, but what she could see held no clues as to her location. The landscape was bereft of any sign of civilization. No phone poles, no roads filled with late-night travelers, no headlights, no electrical lines or cities or even, she realized suddenly, any traces of civilization. Just…a rolling empty swell of land that seemed to disappear into the black night.

"We're twelve hours out of Memphis, a day out of St. Louis," Jake had said. How could that be true? Surely that was one of the most populated shorelines of the entire Mississippi River. There would be houses. Businesses. People. Lights.

She gripped the rail harder. What if it was true? What if it wasn't a dream or a joke? If she *had* somehow leaped into the past?

Oh, God. Panic started a small tremble that grew inside her. Her normally rational brain took an unexpected turn into a *Twilight Zone* frame of mind. Perhaps she'd soon hear the rat-a-tat-tat of keys typing on some unseen rooftop, informing her she was merely part of some elaborate story, her every move controlled by some twisted, unknown author.

Oh, hell, she thought. That's just crazy talk.

No, there had to be a rational explanation. One she could make sense of. Perhaps she hit her head when she fell in the attic and, like Dorothy, had awoken in Oz. And Jake and the pug-faced man and Petunia were merely figments of her overactive imagination. And all it would take would be one swirling ride on a hot-air balloon—if she could only find one—to get her the hell off this freak show and back to Aunty Em…er, Dane. Perhaps, à la Dorothy, there was some great lesson she needed to learn from all this. Like There's No Place Like Home. But now, looking out into the bleak gray beyond the rail of this boat, she could not imagine what that lesson might be.

On the other hand, there was that picture.

Ellie stared down into the black water moving swiftly below the bow. If she jumped in, could she swim to shore from here? How far was it? And once—*if*—she reached the shore, what then? She had no money, no transportation, no phone.

Phone.

Her cell phone! She'd had it in her pocket in the attic. She'd spoken with Bridget just before—

It must have fallen out of her pocket, probably when she was in that wardrobe. If there was a signal—*any signal*—it would prove once and for all that this was just some kind of elaborate prank.

She would call Dane, beg his forgiveness and get herself booked on the next flight out of St. Louis.

She cast one last glance at the lifeboats lashed to the side of the steamer. They looked heavy. Too heavy to manage alone. She filed them mentally in the "last ditch emergency" column and headed back to Jake's window.

It was when she was poised, squirming half in and half out of that devilishly small portal that she felt someone's hands clamp around her ankles and yank her backward.

Fire scraped across the front of her chest as she was dragged along the metal window edge before landing gracelessly on the deck again.

"Ow!"

"Get outta there, ye mangy thief, you!" a man shouted at her, reaching down to clasp one of her hands behind her back to yank her upward.

"Hey!" Ellie yelped as he clapped an arm around her chest, then almost as quickly, released her as if she'd burned through a layer of his skin.

"Holy Jesus, Mary and Joseph! Yer a…a *woman!*"

She rubbed her aching shoulder. "Cleverly deduced, Sherlock. But it's not what it looks like."

"It's Captain to you, ye sneaky little badger."

It wasn't until that moment that she'd noticed he

was dressed in a navy-blue uniform that barely covered his protruding belly. He had a face full of neatly trimmed gray whiskers, and despite or because of that official-looking insignia on his lapel, he was officially peeved.

"Badger?" she repeated warily. Whatever that was, she didn't like the sound of it.

He snatched up her arm again without mercy and shoved her in the direction of the door to his right. "Female or no, I don't tolerate no knucks on my steamer. Ye'd better have a good explanation as to why ye were climbin' in that window, missy. Or you'll be pickin' Mississippi mud from between yer teeth before the night's out."

THREE QUEENS.

A beatable hand, to be sure. But he'd had worse. Jake eyed Bill Jackson as he lowered the corner of his hand back to the table. A man of the cloth, Jackson was well-known to be one of the best gamblers on the circuit and regularly won big pots. His religious affiliation had no apparent influence on his penchant for gambling, nor on his ability to hold his liquor, both of which he'd consumed enthusiastically tonight. In fact, Jake knew, it wasn't usually until his fifth whiskey that the "tell" he normally kept under wraps became apparent. At least, apparent to Jake.

But he'd been reading men since he was eight and living meal-to-meal from refuse stacked in filthy New Orleans alleyways. He was good at it. Which was why, though no one else seemed to notice the way Jackson's pupils dilated when he was bluffing, Jake raised him two thousand dollars.

The preacher's gaze sharpened and flicked up at Jake, all effects of the whiskey suddenly gone. "That's a real shame, Jake," he said, shoving another three thousand out into the pile. "I hate to take your money, but I'll see your two and raise you one."

Jake grinned and shoved out another thousand onto the swollen pile. "Then, just to ease your conscience, we should end the suspense. *Bill.*" He laid down his hand. "Call."

If he hadn't been watching Bill's expression so closely, he might have missed what was going on right behind the man's head. A working girl named Millie who'd hired on to the *Natchez* in New Orleans as a performer sidled up to a rough-looking gray-haired man Jake had never seen before. The girl was dressed in a flimsy, transparent piece of fluff tucked around a revealing corset and satin bloomers. From which she pulled—

Jake's watch.

Damn the little superforker!

His first impulse was to chase after her and the man she'd given it to, who, even as he watched, was making his way out of the room. His second was to realize there was nowhere for them to go. This boat wouldn't dock for another day or so. Plenty of time to deal with them.

So, the Amazon he'd left locked in his room hadn't been lying about taking the watch after all. That realization presented him with a whole new set of unsettling questions. None of which he could address intelligently now.

Bill Jackson tossed his cards facedown toward the center of the table without a hint of emotion and drew Jake's attention back to the game.

A roar went up from the men around him and a round of applause. He'd won. And the pot was considerable. Though Bill Jackson was a long way from being out of it, he studied Jake in the same way a green mantis might a spider it was about to devour.

"Lucky," Bill murmured.

"Luck has nothing to do with it, Bill," Jake declared as he bent to collect his winnings. "I'm a survivor, like you."

Bill grinned without a hint of friendliness. "Ah, but there's the difference between you and me, my friend. While you think of yourself as a survivor, I think of myself as a winner. 'Through Grace it is already mine.' So sayeth the Lord. Amen."

Jake opened his mouth to reply when a ruckus started at the doorway and the crowd parted to make way for Captain Speary and—

Oh, no.

No, no, no…

Speary hauled her directly to his table, and shoved her forward. Clearly, she had stolen some of his clothes, which he had to admit, looked far better on her than they ever had on him. But her feet were bare and her hair was tousled and curtaining her eyes. Even so, he found himself holding his breath just looking at her.

"Caught this little cherry breakin' in through yer cabin porthole," Speary announced, puffing up with importance. "Says she knows ye."

"Breaking *in?*" he repeated, trying to grasp this.

"Aye, stuck halfway through, kickin' to beat all, she was."

"Hey!" she complained, tossing her hair back off her face. "I was *not* stuck. There was plenty of room."

"So I'm askin' ye plain, Jake. D'ye ken this here badger?"

He had two choices. He could deny he'd ever laid eyes on her before, thereby neatly alleviating himself of any more trouble. Speary would put her off at the next stop or have her arrested. Either way, not his funeral.

Second, he could admit they were...acquainted. That, indeed he had left her locked in his cabin, stranger that she was, and that she had not, in fact, done anything wrong. After all, she had told the truth about the bloody watch.

But another possibility occurred as he stared at her, watching him with an expression he could only describe as imploring. And to be honest, it was the sweetest of all choices. Not only would it solve her immediate problem, it would go a long way to solving his as well.

He got to his feet. "You'd be well advised, Shawn, to unhand the girl. She is my wife."

A collective gasp went up from the onlookers. It was matched in volume only by the lady herself.

"*What?*" The captain gaped at him. "*You? Hitched?* I donna believe it."

Jake shrugged, then leaned close to the captain and whispered, "Take a gander at the ring on her hand if you doubt me."

Speary had trouble closing his mouth at the sight of it. Visa, onto his ploy, responded with a vicious narrowing of her lovely eyes.

"*When,* Jake?" Speary asked when he found his voice. "And how in the hell—"

"She joined me at the last port. I know I should've told you," he said, "paid her fare. And I was planning to do just that after the game tonight. But—" he leaned closer to the captain "—I was hoping to keep our little secret until we reached St. Louis. You know, wedded bliss. And, well, look at her. You would've done the same."

As one, the men in the room turned to study her.

Visa looked positively gob-smacked. She sputtered something unintelligible, and Jake put a hand up to silence her. "I know, darlin'. It all happened pretty fast. She needs time to soak it all in. She probably got a little cabin fever tonight, didn't you, precious? Lock yourself out? Step out for some air?"

"I…I—" she sputtered, her cheeks turning crimson—with anger or joy he couldn't be sure. He took the opportunity to slip a wad of bills into Speary's hand.

"Well…" The captain cleared his throat. "Well, that's different, then. I never thought I'd live long enough to see Jake Gannon a married man. My apologies, ma'am. But ye can see how it looked."

"Oh, it must have been a picture," Jake mused aloud. He nodded to the dealer and said, "Pauly, please put my winnings in the safe for me while I escort my wife back to our cabin. I think she's been through enough for one night. Gentlemen? Shall we reconvene in the morning?"

Amidst the muttering and grumbling, not a man tried to stop him as he wrapped a hand around Visa's—the one with the ring on it—and guided her in the direction of the exit.

"Precious?" she hissed. *"Wife?"*

"Just smile, darlin'. I just saved your pretty behind from a watery grave."

She lifted her chin, taking in the room, then planted a heart-stuttering smile on her face. "Now you're just exaggerating."

"No, I'm not."

"Hyperbole is the vernacular of the ignorant."

"Hyperbo—*what?*"

"My point exactly."

JAKE PACED the tiny interior of his cabin as Ellie reclined on his bed, suddenly exhausted. Time-traveling to another century had that effect, apparently. But none of this was easy to take. Least of all being suddenly paired with this perfectly strange, maddeningly interesting man named Jake Gannon.

The wick of the oil lamp on the wall flickered and cast shadows across his bed. She watched him until it made her dizzy.

"I am engaged, you know," she told him. "To be married. FYI."

"Indeed?" Jake stopped his pacing. "Why didn't he come to your rescue?"

Because he exists in some parallel universe. "Is that what you call what you did?"

"What would you call it?"

"I haven't figured it out yet. Give me a minute. I'll come up with the angle. Because you must have one."

"Who are you really?" he asked, stepping closer. "And what were you doing in my cabin in the middle of the night?"

She sighed. "My name is Ellie Winslow. And I haven't the foggiest idea what I'm doing here in your room. Like I said, one minute I was in Deadwood and the next—"

"So you told me." Jake studied her as if she were a bug he'd just found in his soup. "Did you hit your head? Take a spill?"

"No. Well, yes, technically. But that was a hundred and thirty years from now."

He spun away from her as if it actually hurt his ears to listen. "Now see, it's talk like that—"

"Truth, you mean? If you'd rather I lie, just say so. I'm quite good at it. I am from Hollywood, after all."

He sighed deeply. "Look, Visa—Ellie—whatever your name is—I know you didn't take the watch."

"Wow." She sat up. "That must have stung a bit to admit. How did you find out?"

"I saw the girl who forked it pass it to the man who hired her to steal it."

This was getting good. "Who?"

"Never laid eyes on him before. But I can guess who he works for."

"Who? I mean, he works for someone? Why would someone want to target your watch specifically?"

Studying her from under a sweep of long lashes, he unbuttoned his vest and tugged it off. Then he started on the buttons of his shirt. "That's not important."

Oh, but it was. She could tell. Ellie's breath caught. If she had her camera right now, if she could catch that look on film—that dark, brooding sensuality that shadowed his eyes and carved his expression with such a dichotomy of mistrust and vulnerability—that complete unawareness of how he looked—he would be a movie star before the tabloid ink dried. Actors who had it made millions.

Men like Jake, in real life, were, on the other hand, usually trouble. And despite the fact that he had dragged his gaze from hers, she found herself unable to stop looking at the man. Watching the train wreck. Oh, and she could feel the tracks of her life rattle with warning.

He divested himself of the shirt after tugging down his suspenders.

"Wait," she blurted, "what are you doing?"

"Going to sleep."

"But it's almost morning." She crabbed backward on the bed against the headboard. "And there's…only one bed. And I'm in it. And we can't share." She said this a bit more urgently than was absolutely required.

He tugged his trousers off and draped them over the chair. Ellie couldn't take her eyes off the way the muscles of his back bunched under the thin fabric of his long johns.

"I'm tired. And you're making my head hurt. I've told them you're my wife, so we'll have to make the best of it. If you insist, there's plenty of floor for you. Just take a pillow and a blanket and—"

"Hmm," she marveled. "So much for the myth of the Old West and men being gentlemen."

A grin tipped the corners of his mouth. "The bed's big enough for two. Your choice." He blew out the lamp, plunging the room into a gray shadow.

"I am *not* sleeping with you. I don't even *know* you. And…and we're not finished talking yet."

He climbed into the bed and slid under the sheets on the right side of the bed. "Yes, we are."

She scuttled far to the left. "I didn't just fall off the turnip truck, you know, pal. I've been around."

"That certainly instills confidence." He curled into a fetal ball and punched down his pillow. "Try not to fall anymore tonight until we sort this out."

The quiet stretched out between them. Ellie wrapped her arms around her knees, unsure what to do. How to be. She listened to the sound of his breathing, but he seemed to be holding himself as rigidly as she was. Staring into the darkness ahead of him, he finally spoke.

"Do you intend to sit there all night like a propped-up log?"

"Possibly."

He punched his pillow again. "I've never had to force a woman and I'm not about to start tonight. So get off your high horse." He went quiet again for a few seconds. "If there's sex between us, and," he added, "I predict there will be, it'll be because you're begging me for it. Not the other way round." He allowed those words to hang in the air before continuing. "And if you're contemplating sneaking about again, I'd reconsider. A ring like the one you're wearing might just be worth your life in a place like this."

Shocked by his words, Ellie curled her hand into a fist, turning the ring inward toward her palm. So it was about the ring. She should have known. She tipped her head back against the wall, plotting her next move.

Much later she heard his breathing settle into the soft, rhythmic sound of sleep.

Beg him for it. Hah! That'll be the day.

Just how long would she be safe with a man like Jake Gannon? She pulled a blanket up around her, tugged Reese's photo out of her pocket and stared at it in the dim light. *Where the hell are you, Reese? And what are you doing in this crazy picture? And why am I here?*

None of those answers came to her as she watched her erstwhile rescuer sleep, vowing to stay awake and keep her eye on him as the sky outside the window lightened to a dusky blue.

5

IT MIGHT HAVE BEEN the sunlight that woke her, pouring in as it was like a laser beam through the window, scorching her left eye.

Or the sound of the people milling on the deck beyond, talking over the rhythmic sound of the paddle wheel with its back-and-forth sound.

It might have been.

More likely, she decided—acutely aware of the hand curled around her breast—it was the stranger fully spooned against her that had driven her to full wakefulness. That, and the fact that his "morning hello" was pressed into the small of her back.

Ellie covered her face with her hands.

Even worse, she had not woken up from this disaster. She was still in 1876. With…him.

Somehow, in her dream, she'd imagined it was Dane holding her. Even though Dane liked his space when he slept. Didn't like being touched at all. Who would have guessed Jake was a cuddler? And even if she gave him the benefit of the doubt that he'd unconsciously breached the blanket wall she'd erected last night, there was no denying that she'd let him.

Carefully, she lifted his fingers and the dead weight of his arm and eased out from his embrace. She leaned against the wall, studying him as he slept.

Asleep, he seemed less menacing than he had last night. There was even something…well, kind of charming about the way his lips curved upward without his permission. And the uncalculated look morning stubble lent to his jaw.

She wondered about him. Who was he? Moreover, why was she here with him? Was there some reason she'd been flung backward in time to this tiny room floating down the Mississippi? Might she have just as easily landed in some other person's wardrobe? But she hadn't. She had landed in his.

On the other hand, it seemed more than likely this was some gigantic cosmic mistake.

The whole concept baffled her. What if there were a reason for her to have come specifically here? To him. What if some destiny pulled her here so that he might help her find Reese? And now that some of the cobwebs had been cleared from her brain, finding Reese was exactly what she decided she had to do.

Jake's fingers stretched out across the bedding in search of her. He yawned and opened one eye.

Contact.

Finding her watching him, he jerked upright and rubbed a hand down his face, then grumbled some unintelligible oath.

"Morning to you, too," she said.

Scowling, he balled his fingers into a fist, then rubbed his head. "Sorry. I was hoping it was all a bad dream."

She nodded sympathetically. "Listen, I've been thinking…if we change boats in St. Louis, do you think we could catch one that would eventually put us on the path to Deadwood?"

He actually winced. *"We?"*

"Yes. You and me."

Narrowing a look at her, he asked, "And why would we…I do such a thing?"

She dug under her pillow for the picture of Reese and handed it to him. "To find her."

He studied the sepia-toned photograph. His lips parted with what she could only guess was surprise, but then he shrugged. "I don't know her."

"She's my sister. And she needs my help."

"And that's supposed to mean exactly what to me?"

Ellie sighed. "She's also from 2009. Like me."

His answering ten-second you-are-completely-insane stare made her look away.

"You don't believe me. That's okay. I had trouble believing I'm here, too. But it's true. I have fallen through some hole in time. Into this…this mess of a century."

Jake rolled off the bed and headed to the water basin and pitcher poised on a small marble-topped mahogany cabinet. He poured some water into the bowl and proceeded to drown himself in it. Face-first.

"Very funny!" she called to him over the sound of gurgling water. At which point he came up for air and shook his shaggy head, spraying her with cool droplets.

"Sometimes," he said, "I forget when I've had too much to drink. It's only this infernal pounding at the back of my head and the desire to…make some logical sense of my world that I calculate I've overstepped my limits. I suspect that is the case now. Because I thought you said you were from 2009."

"I did say that," she answered. "And I am."

A slow disappointment rolled across his face—as if he'd only just noticed she was a simpleton. "As in…" he ventured, "the future? Some hundred and thirty-three years from…now?"

"That's right."

"And you expect me to what? Believe you?"

Ellie got up and crossed the room to stand toe-to-toe with him. "Frankly, it doesn't really matter if you do or not. But if you really think I can be mistaken for a nine-teenth-century woman, then you haven't been paying attention. I know things. Things you can't possibly know."

He lifted a brow. "Such as?"

She searched through the kaleidoscopic knowledge of history she'd accumulated as a brief history major at Brown. "Well, such as…in 1876, the election of Ruther-ford B. Hayes as president of the United States will happen due to overnight crafty electoral politicking by some superdelegates. He will lose the popular vote, but will win nonetheless, a result that will be oddly mirrored some hundred and twenty-two years from now."

She smiled. "And the same Sioux that will soon defeat General George Custer at the Bighorn River? They'll go practically extinct by the late 1800s as the U.S. Government all but annihilates them and imprisons them on reservations out of fear and massive, intoler-ant greed."

He shook his head. "Custer? Defeated? That's not likely. Besides, I hear the Sioux Nations are banding together—"

"It won't matter. They're finished. Not even their Ghost Dances will save them. *That* isn't until the 1890s." Jake looked confused, but she went on. "Until, of course, one of them has the brilliant idea sometime in the 1980s to build a casino on the rez and make a little dough. Then the U.S. can't tax them fast enough. Oh, a cute invention called the automobile will replace the horse in only a few years. Men will fly in airplanes around the world and in spaceships to the moon and back."

"Air *what?* That," he said with a scowl, "is the most fanciful piece of bunkum I've ever—"

She pulled her credit card from her pocket. "What if I told you that this piece of plastic could buy me just about anything I wanted halfway around the world in a matter of seconds?"

A pause ensued as he tried to imagine it. "Let 'er rip," he demanded. "Show me."

She faltered. "In 2009. *Not now.* It requires satellites, fiber optic cables, computers."

"As I thought," he declared, reaching for his pants and tugging them on. Then he opened the wardrobe doors and pulled out his boots.

What did it really matter, she thought, turning toward the daylight spilling in the porthole window. She wouldn't convince him. He thought she was crazy. And really, who could blame him? She had no real proof and the story was…well, you just couldn't make that stuff up. Still, his arrogance irked her.

"You know," she said quietly, staring out the window at the people on the deck, "my story may seem far-fetched to you. But we're not so different, you know. I mean, have you ever tried to explain to someone how you do what you do? Can you explain what makes you a good card player?"

"I'm not good. I'm the best," he stated, pulling on his boot.

Nor was his ego in need of stroking. "But can you explain how you anticipate how men bet? How you—" she hesitated "—know when to hold 'em and when to fold 'em?"

He didn't answer. Outside the window, she saw the captain, who met her eyes as he passed by Jake's cabin. He touched the brim of his hat to her and went on his way. Ellie smiled in return.

"You can't explain those things," she murmured, "because they're intangibles. You take them on faith."

Something made her turn then, to find that Jake had gone very still with his back toward her. He was staring at something in his hands. Slowly, and with a puzzled expression, he faced her, holding her cell phone in his hands. "This, I presume, belongs to you?"

"Yes!" She'd completely forgotten the phone in all the chaos last night. She leaped to him and grabbed it out of his hands. The tears threatening only moments earlier flowed in earnest now. Oh! She never thought she'd be so happy to see a stupid cell phone in her life.

He took a suspicious step back from her as she twirled once like a six-year-old with a new video game, then settled back on the bed to see if it worked. The screen was an ominous black, and the glass casing had shattered, probably when she landed on it. Still, she pushed the power button, praying it would come on.

"What is that...thing?" he asked.

"A phone. You call people with it. Take pictures, Google restaurant locations. Check your e-mail."

He had no idea what she was talking about. She knew that. But she couldn't help but be giddy over proving herself to him.

He rubbed at the back of his neck and started pacing again. "You and I are nothing alike. I've spent a lifetime learning to do what I do. Hard work. It has no relation to faith whatsoever. You, on the other hand, expect me to believe something entirely unbelievable simply because—"

"It's broken."

"—because you say it's so." He stopped to look at her as she punched the power button repeatedly. "What?"

"It's broken. It won't work." Disappointment made her limbs feel completely leaden.

He simply nodded, shrugging on his coat. "I'm going to get us some food. I think you need something to eat."

"Don't patronize me," she spat. "Believe me or don't. But I know you've never seen anything like this before."

His eyes roved over her, not the device in her hands. With a regretful shake of his head, he muttered, "You're quite right, Visa. I never have."

NICHOLAS TELBY SAT in the dark shelter of his cabin fingering the watch Millie had forked for him last night.

The gold lid was smooth with years of wear and the insidious ticking sound filled the silent room. On the inside lid, cut into the soft metal, were etched the words he'd suspected he'd find there. The words that proved what he and the others had guessed already. That Jake Gannon was not who he claimed to be.

The inscription was worn, as if someone had rubbed it off over the years. But the lettering was still there: "To my husband, Thomas Kane, with devotion, your Jessie."

There was only one way this particular watch could've fallen into Jake Gannon's hands: Thomas and Jessie's son, Ezra Kane. Because the man who'd once owned it was long dead now. As was the woman who'd inscribed it with her name.

He lifted a quill pen from the holder on the small desk nearby and drew a piece of paper from the drawer. He began to write. Tomorrow they would dock at the wood-filling station and he would telegram his partners the news. The credit for the find would belong to him. He was, after all, the one who'd found Gaines or Gannon or whatever he was calling himself these days. And that was the curious thing about them all, Telby mused, scribbling his name to the note and stamping the ink with the rocker blotter to dry it. No matter where they tried to hide, their past inevitably caught up with them. As surely as it just had with the boy who'd ridden beside the vicious William Quantrell, Jackson Gaines.

As HE CONTEMPLATED his next move, Jake wrapped his hands around the wooden rail at the edge of the deck. He watched a flock of sand cranes lift off the water in an elegant white wedge, their wings beating in unison, their purpose synchronized. The coming of winter had sent most of them south. Farther west, on the Platte and the Big Blue, he'd seen them so thick in the sky they nearly blotted out the sun. They were creatures of habit. Fly north in the summer, south in the winter. They mated, bore young and did it all over again. Never questioning that pattern.

Watching them, he found himself longing for such simplicity in his own life. Not a family or children—those he would never have—but the comfort of knowing your destination. Just once, he thought, he'd like to know. But chaos like Visa always seemed to derail his most well-laid plans. Even he had to admit, though, she would puzzle a Philadelphia lawyer. Either she was crazy, or he was. Because that smashed-up device she'd shown him had begun to make him question his own sanity.

It was true he'd never seen, or, for that matter, touched anything like it. But that didn't make it what she claimed. Nor did the fact that whenever he looked at her directly, rational thought tended to scatter faster than buckshot. Even now, he felt himself go hard at the thought of her. But he could think of simpler ways to kill himself, if that's what he truly wanted.

But what really concerned him wasn't that she seemed hell-bent on finding that sister of hers, a task for which she seemed about as prepared as a newborn pup. No, what concerned him was that he found himself wanting to, somehow, protect her from herself.

He shook his head, staring down at the water sliding by the hull of the steamer, and he reminded himself about the ring. A thing like that could straighten his situation out in no time and then some. A ring like that could change his life. Maybe there was a deal to be struck. Maybe that was his destination.

From the corner of his eye, he spotted the petite mousy-haired pickpocket, Millie, who'd visited him last night. He ground his teeth together, then followed her.

Walking purposefully toward the stern, she caught sight of him and made a sharp left into the hallway that led to the casino, where a noisy crowd promised haven. But he was too fast for her. He grabbed her arm and jerked her into the alcove of a doorway, out of sight of the men in the room beyond.

Jake pressed her backward against the doorway and trapped her there with his arm against her throat.

"Where's the watch you forked last night, Millie?"

She threw her head back and made as if to scream. He clapped a hand over her mouth instead.

Two days ago he might have called her pretty. But his standard of "pretty" had just been racheted up considerably in the past twenty-four hours. She had bad skin—a far cry from Visa's flawless complexion—but a pleasant enough face, hair that haloed her in a wreath of curls and reminded him of a dog he'd once owned in color and texture. "It's a long way to shore," he whispered in her ear. "Can you swim?"

She shook her head, her coffee-colored eyes wide.

"That's a real shame," he said. "Now, tell me the name of the man you gave it to." He lifted his hand off her mouth.

"I didn't fork your bloody watch—"

He covered her mouth again and dragged her toward the end of the corridor toward the ship's rail. She screamed into his palm and bucked in his arms.

"What? You say you want to tell now?"

She nodded against his hand. When he released her, she spat onto the deck and sent him an evil look. "See here, you've made my lip bleed," she complained, dabbing it with her tongue.

"The cold water should take care of it." He jerked her forward again, but she stopped him.

"All right, ya brute. His name's Nicholas Telby. He's new to the card room. Must'a got on just recent. Promised me cash. A gold eagle, as if it's any concern of yours. But he burned me. Only gave me five."

"Why'd he want my watch?"

She snorted. "Why would he tell me that? All he says is to get it. Nothin' else. Just the watch—like it were special to him." She plucked at the bodice of her lowcut dress, straightening it out. "Haven't seen him since I gave it over to him. And good riddance. There's somethin' off with that burner."

"Such as?"

"I mean," she elaborated, "any man who done what he done to Leanne last night should be strung up by his you-know-what and left to rot."

Jake felt his face go hot. Leanne was a friend of his, formerly a prostitute who'd worked Shawn's card room for the past few years. She'd stopped making a living on her back after Shawn heard her sing. Since then, she'd been his opening act.

"What happened to her?"

The woman swallowed hard. "He chewed her up. Broke her cheek. And that's only the half of it. I don't give a fig about my gold eagle. He can keep his damned money. I'm well out."

She probably had no idea how right she was. "I catch you anywhere near my room again, and I'll make good on my threat. Do we understand each other?"

She nodded. "Sorry about yer watch. It weren't nothin' personal, Mr. Gannon."

But it was, he thought, watching her hurry down the hall away from him. It was very personal, indeed. He turned in the other direction and headed off to find Leanne.

Tired of waiting for Jake to return, Ellie had left his room to explore on her own and frankly found the facilities severely lacking. The crude restroom consisted of a splintery board with a hole, which, if one were not very careful, could lead to an untimely plunge into the chilly Mississippi. There were a few tubs standing in the middle of the room, but no sign to segregate it by gender and a wide-open doorway that allowed for zero privacy.

She ran into the captain on the foredeck of the ship as she stood staring at the shoreline, speculating about her swimming abilities. Speary's already blustery face reddened when she spoke to him, and he repeatedly made a stab at taming his wild gray hair with his hand as they spoke. This encounter was considerably more amicable than the last one. He apologized for the misunderstanding the previous night and asked if there was anything he could do to make it up to her.

"Captain Speary," she said, "there is one thing and only one thing you could do to earn my forgiveness."

The captain's face brightened. "What's that?"

"A bath. A long, hot bath in my room. Is that even possible?"

"It is no' only possible, lass," he replied. "It shall be done in the next ten minutes."

Now, Ellie sat and leaned against the warm backrest of the antique hip-bath Speary had ordered brought to her room and filled with steaming water. She played with the milky bubbles she'd made of soap and felt herself relax for the first time in twenty-four hours.

The heat of the water seeped into her tired muscles. She couldn't help but make comparisons to the tub in her real bath—the one with jets and the infinity edge that sounded like a waterfall. Still, the simplicity of this one made her grateful. If she had to live for a while in the nineteenth century, at least she wouldn't have to entirely give up the necessities of life. Besides, she would return to the future. She would find a way to get there. She'd find Reese, and together they'd figure it out. If they could be thrown back in time, then why not forward?

Ellie closed her eyes and tried to recall every second before she'd awoken in Jake's wardrobe. The trunk. All the treasures, books, the photograph. That's where the secret lies, she thought. That picture moved. No one would ever convince her otherwise, as unlikely as that was. But how? And how had it found its way into a trunk in her grandmother's attic? And that camera they hadn't spotted earlier…

And what about the man at the premiere? What did he have to do with it and was he connected somehow to this?

Those questions swam around and around in her mind until her brain hurt. Then she heard a knock at the door.

"Visa?"

It was Jake. She closed her eyes. "It's *El-lie*."

A strained pause. *"Ellie?"*

"Go away."

One-one-hundred, two-one-hundred, three…

"This is my room."

She bit back a smile. "*Our* room. We're married, remember? Now go away."

Seconds ticked by, during which she wondered if she only imagined smoke pouring in under the door. "I'm coming in."

"What? No!" She ducked under the water to her chin. "Don't you dare!"

But he gave no second warning. He just opened the door and barged right in.

He stopped short and frowned at the sight of her. "How the hell did *that* get in here?"

She sank lower, up to her lips. "The captain."

"Speary?"

She nodded.

He narrowed his eyes. "Really."

"Is that all you have to say? How about 'Oops! Excuse me. Didn't mean to barge in on you. I'll be going now…'"

Dropping a tapestry bag on the floor and a box of something that smelled rather tasty on the bedside table, he settled himself down on the bed and crossed his arms, watching her. There was something unsettling in his look, something…angry.

"I suppose the good captain probably read your mind…or somehow prestidigitated that thing in here, steamin' water and all. I mean with your magic powers and bein' from the future and such."

She scowled at him. "Now you're just mocking me."

He scratched his jaw, his stubbly beard making a raw sandpapery sound. "Then I assume that means you left this room when I told you not to."

"Hey, I'm not your prisoner. I'm your pretend wife. I can go where I want, when I want."

"That so?" He gestured at the door. "Be my guest, then."

She sank lower, tightening her arms over her breasts.

"No, I mean it. You're so all-fired anxious to find yourself trouble, be my guest." He swept a hand toward the door again.

She glared at her French pedicured toes peeking out of the water.

"No?" he inquired, leaning forward. "Then maybe it's time for some straight talk. Just between you and me."

Ellie had been pinned to the wall by the best. Journalists, detectives, paparazzi. But he had her. Naked. In a bathtub.

"What do you want from me?" she asked. "I've told you everything I—"

"I want the truth. What's your connection to Nicholas Telby and what were you really doing in my room last night?"

"Nicholas Telby?" Taken aback by Jake's sudden

shift, she didn't even know what to say. "I have no idea who—"

"Tell me plain, Ellie. And don't give me any more claptrap about the future or Rutherford B. Hayes or any other lies that pop up in that demented imagination of yours."

"Demented!"

"Yes, demented. And devious."

Oh! The insufferable nerve of him! "I suppose you think I'm happy about this hideous turn of events! I suppose you think you're the only one who's a little put out here."

His volume rose. "You're the interloper here, not me. I was just going about my own life here when—"

She wanted to stick her fingers in her ears and sing *"La-la-la-la"* but instead she held her breath and ducked underwater. She couldn't take him or his arrogant condescension anymore. Let him rant and rave. She didn't have to hear it.

But after a few seconds he reached in and tugged her up by the wrist. She gasped and slapped his hand away. "Don't touch me!"

"I can outwait you. We can sit here until the water goes ice cold. But you are going to tell me what you know."

She swiped at the water sheeting down her face and cowered there, hating him. Wishing she could be somewhere, anywhere, else. "I don't know this man Telby— whoever he is—and I told you *everything* I know about what I'm doing here, which is essentially nothing. You're going to have to decide once and for all if you believe what I told you or not because I'll never be able to prove it to you—phone or no phone."

Her voice broke, but she went on. "But that's really your problem, isn't it, Jake? You don't trust anyone or anything. You think you can bully and bluff your way through life like it was one big poker game. Well, guess what? This time you can't!"

She was starting to shiver now. And more horrifying, tears were stinging the backs of her eyes. But it didn't matter. "Whatever happened to you out there today, whatever has put you in this mood has nothing to do with me. I don't care if you help me or not. And if you don't believe me, then fine. I have never meant you any harm. But I won't let you bully me. I'll go, and we'll never see each other again. And that's fine with me. I'll make it on my own."

He scowled at her. She'd stung him. But not enough to get him out of the room.

"Did you hear me? *Get out.*"

Still he didn't move. He simply stared at her, as if there was some two-sided conversation going on in his mind about her sanity. But she'd be damned if she'd let him keep her cowering in this water another minute. So she did the only thing she could think of that would give her any power at all.

She stood up.

Jake's expression flattened with shock, and his gaze, which had strayed downward, jerked back up to her face.

Dripping wet, with soapsuds still sliding down the curves of her naked breasts and hips, she lifted her chin and pointed at the door. "Get. Out."

Jake took an uncertain step, then did what she'd asked. Ellie managed to wait until she heard his footsteps disappear down the hallway before she covered her face with her hands and cried.

6

As THE WHISTLE of the *Natchez* blew a long, harmonic note, Jake downed a shot of whiskey at a table tucked in the corner of the card room. He frowned down at the ring of moisture it left on the *Memphis Appeal* newspaper someone hadn't bothered to take with them. For the past hour he'd made a serious attempt to drink away the empty feeling he'd left the room with, but so far whiskey had done nothing to fill up that particular hole.

Damn the woman. What did he care if she fled? Standing up naked as a dove—had she done it just to shock him? Or was her intention to hornswoggle him? He ran his finger across the damp top of the glass, making a high-pitched sound. What did he care if she chased after her damned sister and got herself killed? Or worse.

She wasn't his problem. She was merely a passing headache. Let her find her way up to Deadwood, he told himself. A woman like that…

That's your problem, isn't it, Jake? You don't trust anyone or anything. You think you can bully or bluff your way through life like it was a poker game…

He shook his head. Bully? Nobody'd ever called him that before. He poured himself another glass of whiskey.

Was he?

He tossed back the shot and felt the whiskey scald its way satisfyingly down his throat. It was possible he'd crossed a line back there, threatening her. He'd like to meet the man who would trust a woman who claimed to be from another century with far-fetched tales of flying to the moon and back. Hell, even *he* could make up stories that sounded more convincing than that.

But seeing Leanne this morning had put an edge on him. She'd refused to let him in at first, but finally admitted that the beating Telby had given her had everything to do with her knowing Jake and what information she could give up on him. In the end all she'd been able to tell the man was that she'd never let Jake pay her, and that they were friends. But about his past, she knew nothing, like everyone else. And for that, Telby had broken her cheek and taken his piece for free.

And one more thing. He'd said something she didn't fully understand. Something about how he'd be paid well, no matter what she knew because he had another source of information.

Even now, it made Jake want to kill the son of a bitch. It would be simple enough to tell Speary what happened, implicate Telby. Leanne never would; she was too scared. But if he did it, no doubt whatever Telby knew about Jake would become public knowledge. That he wouldn't risk.

Which brought him back to the auburn-haired woman in his room.

His thoughts kept stalling on the sight of her standing

naked in that tub, her gray eyes full of hurt and vinegar. Just like a woman as pretty as her to use that on him. She was something, crazy or not.

He poured another drink, but stopped the glass halfway to his mouth. That right there, he mused, was a slippery slope, trying to separate the woman from the crazy, or duty from choice.

Some things you have to take on faith.

Her words kept rolling back to him like the sea. *Faith.* For him that word came with a tangle of strings attached to it and put him in mind of a day, long, long ago, when he'd still believed in things. A bloody, long-ago day. And then there was the matter of that photograph.

Onstage, Millie was singing something about a parasol and a park. She avoided looking at him.

"You readin' that there paper, sir?" asked a balding, squat man sitting at the table near him. "I'd be obliged to borrow it if'n you're done."

Jake glanced down at the Memphis paper, and made to hand it over.

"Sure," he said. "Sorry about the—"

The headline on the front page stopped him cold. He drew the paper back and blinked at it in disbelief.

Ohio Governor Rutherford B. Hayes Throws Hat into U.S. Presidential Race! He clutched the newspaper tightly and reread it.

What were the odds of her knowing that? He looked at the date at the top of the page. Yesterday. She could have seen it. But when?

He turned to the man beside him. "Had you heard this before? About this Hayes running for president?"

"Ya don't say?" The stranger read the headline and shook his head. "Times keep on changin', don't they? Nothin' ever seems to hold still."

Jake swallowed hard. No, nothing ever did. He snatched the paper back from the man and slipped his hat on. "Sorry," he told him. "I need this."

WHEN HE GOT BACK to the room, she was gone. Cleared out, as if she'd never been there. She'd left his clothes folded neatly on his bed, and the tub was gone, too. For the blink of an eye, he actually felt relieved, as if he'd dodged some falling rock or missed getting run down by trouble.

But that only lasted a moment. Long enough to look out the window and see black clouds rolling in from the west and to realize the engines had stopped their backing and filling. In fact, the steamer had pulled ashore and tied up at some wood-filling station at the edge of a forest in the middle of nowhere.

No, no, no…

He ran out on deck to look for her. She was nowhere. She wouldn't have— Hell, even *she* wouldn't be *that* stupid.

He stopped a woman walking toward the bow holding a small child by the hand, and a man walking alone to ask if they'd seen her. No one had. Jake ran a hand over his mouth and scanned the landscape.

In the distance, half a mile off, a dirty window of rain was bisecting the sky, slanting across the grassland with uncommon fury. To the east, where the dock was, a broad slope of land was covered with hickory, elm and oaks. On the north, a lonely road wound up over the grassy hilltop above the filling station and disappeared over the horizon.

If he went after her, he'd likely be left behind. If he didn't—

Dammit.

He had no real choice, did he? After all, he was the one who'd driven her to run. If he hadn't pushed her—

He might just make it if he ran like hell and caught her before she got too far. So he started running. He leaped off the deck onto the uneven, floating dock and hurried down to the collection of shacks at the end, past the parade of men wheeling carts full of wood onboard. The place consisted of not much more than a stable of a rangy string of horses, a telegraph office and a small eatery.

A bearded old man dressed in greasy buckskins was too busy giving directions to bother much with him.

"Please," Jake asked, "did a woman pass by here? Tall, beautiful, dressed in men's britches?"

"Had a feller wantin' to send a telegraph, that's all. Folks is too busy nowadays to bother conversin' with an old codger likes o' me."

Telegraph? A warning prickled through him. "What man?" Jake demanded.

"What?" The man scratched his dirty hair, then casually opened his palm. "Oh, that's against reg-alations, to di-vulge such things as—"

Jake pressed a dollar into his wrinkled hand. The old man looked down at it and back up at Jake, waiting. Jake pressed another two in his palm. The coins jangled together as he clutched them in his hand.

"Name was…lemme see…a feller name of Telby. That's what he signed it. You know him?"

The possibilities of the situation settled over Jake like a heavy blanket. "Give me a name. Who received it?"

"Now, again, that there's confidential." The old man ran a palm over his beard as a fox might lick his coat. "No, siree, I couldn't part with—"

Jake shoved a gold eagle in his palm.

The old man put it between what was left of his teeth and grinned. "Well, lemme see. I believe he sent it to a feller in St. Louis by the name of Besson. A Mr. Luc Besson at the St. Mark Hotel."

Besson. The very name sent a cold sweat surging across his forehead. It had been years since he'd last heard it, during a chapter of his life he'd thought he'd closed. But it all fell together in his mind as the old man pocketed the coins: Besson, Telby and the watch. And Ellie. Whatever Luc Besson wanted with him, it could only mean one thing—now that Telby had found Jake, Besson would be waiting for him at the end of this line. And Jake would do whatever he could to make sure that wouldn't happen.

Fat droplets of rain smacked him in the face as he turned his attention back to the most pressing matter. "What about the woman? Did you see her? Very tall. Very pretty. Beautiful in fact."

"Well," considered the old man, sending a stream of brown spit into the water off the dock, "if I wuz lookin' for someone fittin' that particular description, I'd be lookin' thata way." He pointed toward the upper deck of the boat. "That the cherry you mean?"

Jake looked back. There she was, watching him from

the upper deck railing as if the wind had lifted her up and set her down there just to spite him. She sent him a hostile little four-fingered wave before straightening like a wronged princess and strolling down the deck of the *Natchez,* and away from him.

"That one was free," the old man said, turning back to his work.

Jake swore. And then the sky opened up.

ELLIE HURRIED toward the front of the boat, dodging passengers, watching the amazing rainstorm that had whipped up the river and darkened the horizon. She had nothing more to say to Jake, really. What could she say? *I'm horrified that I flashed you? I've never done anything like that before in my life?* Or, how about, *The universe is trying to teach me something here, but I'm fairly certain now it doesn't involve you?*

She glanced back to see Jake pushing his way toward her with a look on his face that rivaled the thunderclouds overhead.

"Ellie!" he shouted over the hiss of the rain. "Wait right there!"

She didn't. She kept moving. She wasn't sure, honestly, if she was frightened, or amazed that he was chasing her. She simply hoped he didn't catch her.

But he did. He grabbed her arm and spun her toward him.

"Dammit, Ellie, what're you running from?"

"Let me go!"

He dropped her arm and scraped water off his face with one hand. His shirt was stuck to his skin, his hair flattened to his forehead in what she had to admit was a cute Elvis curl. As he paced beside her, his shoes made suctiony sounds on the wooden deck. "Did you enjoy that? Watching me chase my tail with worry about you?"

"You? Worried for me? Wait! What was that sound?" she asked rhetorically, looking down. "Oh. I think I just heard hell freezing over!"

Scowling, he started after her as she began another fast walk down the hallway. "Well, pardon me for imagining that you did something idiotic, like run off. Because everything else about you makes so much sense."

He skidded to a stop as she turned on him. "If you will recall the aforementioned 'turnip truck' from which I did not fall? That still applies. What kind of an idiot would I have to be to go wandering off on my own in the middle of nowhere? And because of you? Wow. Your ego is seriously in need of a reality check."

"My *what?*"

"Ego, my friend. And why were you running after me, anyway? I'm a liar, remember? In cahoots with what's his name—your arch enemy? And clearly responsible for all your current problems."

He ducked his head, slapping the soaked rolled newspaper in his hands against his thigh with a little *splat, splat, splat* as a pair of passengers strolled past them, arm in arm under the portico cover, dry as camels.

The *Natchez*'s whistle sounded with an earsplitting noise. On the dock the haulers had finished loading wood and were throwing off the heavy lines, even as the steamer moved away from the shore.

"I might have been…" The rest was lost to a mumble into his hand.

"What?" she asked, bending closer. "I didn't catch that."

"Back in the room. I might have been…hasty to accuse you."

His words actually stunned her. "Wa-was that actually an apology?"

"You might be obliged to put it like that," he muttered, staring out at the rain pockmarking the river. The sound of it clattered against the roof above them and splattered against the nearby rail. Most of the sane people scurried indoors, off the deck.

"What miracle brought this on? This sudden change of heart?"

He glanced down for a protracted minute at the soggy newspaper in his hand, then tossed it overboard into the water. It floated on the current until it disappeared under the steamer's churning wake. "Maybe I just changed my mind," he replied. He looked at her and frowned. "Have you been crying?"

"What? *No.*" She touched her puffy eyes. "God, no, it's just the smoke from the wood they're burning below. Stings my eyes. You were saying?"

Clearly, he didn't believe her. But his next words were quiet, almost tender. "What exactly were you planning to do if you didn't stay with me? Sleep on deck?"

"What do you care?" She turned to go, but he caught her by the arm and, steering them into an alcove, pulled her back until she was flat up against him.

"Who says I do?" he asked, his mouth close to hers.

With his eyes, he traced the shape of her lips like a man searching a map for something he'd lost.

Ellie held her breath, shocked to find herself in his arms. Shocked to realize that this sensation felt foreign and good; the thought of pushing him away, the furthest thing from her mind.

And then he kissed her. Softly the first time, a tentative slide of his mouth against hers with his eyes open, watching her. She was watching him, too, wondering what she was doing. Wondering at the softness of his lips and thinking that she shouldn't let this happen.

Then he covered her mouth with his and she forgot to warn herself. He slid his hand behind her head and his fingers into her hair and she found herself doing the same. He tasted of whiskey and rain and need.

She'd never been kissed like this before.

Oh, she'd been kissed, but not with the soul-wrenching hunger of this kiss. Not with the feeling that she might, if she were not very careful, never want to come up for air.

But Jake did. He lifted his mouth from hers and looked at her darkly before pulling her farther into the recesses of a doorway out of sight from the few people left on deck. He pressed himself against her, twining his fingers in hers as he pressed her hands behind her, trapping her there against the door. She could feel his need for her. And hers for him hovered somewhere low and tight in her belly—a sudden desire for this physical contact with him that made her lean toward him. But he stayed just out of reach, watching her as if she were some butterfly specimen he'd captured in his hands.

"Is this about the bathtub?" she asked, "because if it is—"

"No. Yes. Not exactly."

Not exactly? "What exactly is it?"

"I don't know," he said, watching her mouth, then tasting her throat with the tip of his tongue, just beneath her ear.

A tremor rocketed through her. She seemed to have no control over her reaction to him.

"Ohh," she murmured, "you shouldn't do that."

"No?" He traced the side of her neck to her collarbone with his mouth, leaving a trail of moisture behind that aroused her.

"No. Definitely…absolutely—" a sigh tumbled out of her "—not."

"Why? Because you're spoken for?" He loosened his hand and slid it down her arm and across her breast, then around the side of her ribs until he'd pulled her even closer to him, so she could feel his erection.

There was no missing it.

"Yes, because of that—" she tipped her head back, allowing him full access to the small dip between her collarbone "—and because," she murmured, "I'm still…mad at you."

"Ellie…" he breathed.

"What?"

"You make me lose my head around you."

Something about his admission touched her. The feeling was definitely mutual. "I do?"

"Mmm-hmm," he answered, pulling her up hard against him one last time before he turned her loose and took a step back. "But that's a dangerous thing. For both of us."

Shaken and breathing hard, she hesitated, but started to reach out to him, then stopped herself. "That's pretty cle—"

"There's something I haven't told you."

"What?"

"That photograph of yours?" he said, staring out at the rain sweeping geometric designs on the surface of the river. "The one with that woman you claim is your sister? I know that man who's standing beside her."

7

"His name's Sam Keegan," Jake stated, examining the photo of Reese and the stranger as they sat on the edge of his bed. "I knew him a long time ago. Years. I didn't want to believe it at first when I saw that picture."

"My God, Jake," she said, feeling as if some bloom was spreading open inside her. "Do you know what this means? It means it's not random at all."

"What isn't?"

"My coming here. My showing up here, in your cabin. Because you're involved. You're part of it somehow. You can help me find them."

"No." He stood and began pacing again. "No."

"Why not?"

"Because I wouldn't know where to look. I've only seen Sam once in all these years since the war." Jake stood and unbuttoned his soaking-wet shirt and stripped it off.

"The Civil War?"

"The Conflict, yes. It was," he said, starting on the buttons of his long johns, "an ugly time. I don't like to remember it." He dried himself off with a towel on the washstand. She heard the scrape of the soft cotton against his stubbled jaw as he brought the towel to his face and rested it there for a minute.

"But…you must have been so young. Just a boy."

He nodded, not looking at her.

"That's terrible." She'd heard such things, but it was hard to imagine she was here talking to a veteran of the Civil War, one who had fought beside men twice his age. "So you and this Sam got pulled into the war and you fought for what? The North or the South?"

When his eyes rose to meet hers, there was something close to devastation there. "South," he answered. "And I wasn't conscripted. I signed up."

"Didn't your parents try to stop you?"

An ironic smile lifted one side of his mouth. "If I'd had any, I suppose they might have tried. It was," he allowed, "an ill-considered decision." He motioned with his finger for her to turn around as he began unbuttoning his soaked pants.

Ellie scooted back on the bed and kept her attention on the wall, away from him. "And you haven't seen Sam since the war?"

"Once. Years ago. He was headed out west."

"West? But where is he now? You never hear from him?"

"I move around a lot."

She snuck a glimpse of him as he pulled on dry pants. She couldn't help it. He had a beautiful ass framed by a perfect lean yet muscled body, but for the scar on his upper arm—which she only noticed just now. It looked like a burn. It had been a nasty one, too. Something broke inside her as she wondered how he'd gotten it.

As he straightened, she dropped her attention to the photograph again, embarrassed that she'd invaded his privacy. His scars were none of her business, nor was the punch of desire she felt as she watched him. Back home, her fiancé waited, not even knowing what had happened to her. None of this was fair.

Reese's face, captured in the grainy image, seemed to be laughing at her and her inability to puzzle this out. And Sam Keegan, he was handsome but stoic-looking. As if, like Jake, he had many secrets to keep. She ran her fingers over the photo, then because she had no other safe place to land her gaze, she turned the photo over. On the back was a stamp and a signature, terribly faded, but almost legible.

"Ezra Kane," she read aloud. Why did that name sound so weirdly familiar to her?

"What did you say?" Jake asked, his focus suddenly on her.

"The photographer. His name here looks like Ezra Kane. Isn't that a strange na—"

Jake snatched the photo from her hands and studied the photographer's stamp.

"What is it? What's wrong?" she asked.

Obviously troubled, Jake handed her back the photograph and sank down on the bed. "You asked me why I accused you, why I suspected you of working with Telby."

She didn't answer, she just waited.

"When I saw Sam in your photograph, I thought it was a setup. I thought Telby or the man he's working for had sent you in to prove—" He stopped short of finishing and stared at his hands. "The watch that girl stole? It belonged once to Ezra and before that, his father. He gave it to me. We're…old friends."

It was good to know that Jake wasn't alone in this world, that he had friends he cared about. "Why would Telby want it?"

"Telby didn't. The man he's working for wanted it."

"Jake, you're not making any sense."

"His name is Luc Besson. I rode with him once. In a time in my life I try hard to forget. He's a cold-blooded killer. He'll kill for the sheer pleasure of doing it."

"How do you know it's him that's after you? And why would he want to kill you?"

"Telby sent a telegraph to him back there. As to why? Your guess is as good as mine. I just know we should cut a wide path around him."

"So are we clear," she asked, "you understand that I'm not involved in this? In setting you up? Or stealing your watch."

He shook his head. "You're either the best burner alive, or the unluckiest female I ever met. Either way, I conceive I'd as soon throw my hat in with you as with them."

Will miracles never cease? "What changed your mind?"

He reached for a fresh shirt from the closet and slid his arms into it, then slowly buttoned it up. "That thing you were talking about. Instinct. I guess I couldn't really convince myself you were bad."

"Wow." She laughed out loud. "Jake, you really know how to turn a girl's head."

He laughed in return without apology. Picking up a comb, he dispensed with that little Elvis curl, smoothing his hair back so he looked too handsome for her own good.

"Do you know where this Ezra Kane is?" she asked.

He stared in the mirror for a few beats too long. "He might still be in St. Louis, taking pictures. But I haven't talked to him in a few months. He could be anywhere. He gets around."

"St. Louis? Then we should go there first."

"First?"

"Before we go to Deadwood."

"It's a bad idea."

Ellie smoothed her hand over the soft quilt on his bed, for the first time clear there was something else going on here that she didn't understand. "Is it the 'we' part of the idea that's bad? Or going there at all?"

He tossed the comb on the washstand. "Can we talk about this later? I've got a game in a few minutes." He returned to the tapestry bag and handed it to her. "I borrowed these for you. Put 'em on. You'll be less—" his gaze landed on her jeans "—noticeable."

She took the bag as he headed for the door. "We're not done talking about this, you know!" she called as he disappeared from the room.

Ellie opened the tapestry bag and looked in.

"Oh, no."

WHEN SHE CAME OUT, Jake was waiting, propping up a wall across the way. Slowly he straightened as she moved farther into the hallway wearing Leanne's red silk dress like it had never been worn before. For a moment, his blood might have forgotten to flow.

She spread her arms wide and twirled for him.

"You look—" he began.

"—like a soiled dove?" she finished.

"Beautiful." With her hair down like that, tumbling over her nearly bare shoulders, Jake could almost imagine how a man might find it hard to live without her.

She stared down at the full skirt and the sleeveless bodice with its plunging neckline. "I don't know, Jake. This might send the wrong message."

"To who?"

She spread her arms wide. "Exactly."

That made him smile. "C'mon. Let's go earn some money."

"You mean, by gambling?"

"Hell, no. By playing poker. That's no gamble at all. And the way you're dressed—" his gaze traveled over her face slowly "—I don't hardly see how you could bring me anything but luck."

"GANNON, YOU MUST BE the unluckiest card player on the Mississippi River tonight."

Henry Raymond, one of the best on the riverboat circuit, leaned his considerable girth back in his chair and chewed on his stogie with a broad, brown-toothed smile. "Must be the little woman is cramping your style, you reckon?"

"Maybe his luck's just plum run out," said the man at Henry's right elbow, Nicholas Telby. He smiled drunkenly at Jake and raised a shot of bourbon in his direction.

Jake didn't bother looking up. Nor did he look at the beauty pretending to be his wife, who would only distract him with the visible distress on her face. She would make, he decided, a terrible poker player.

One-eyed Charles Llewellen, the man to Jake's left, tipped the bottle's liquid into his own glass with some irritation. "Seems to me, Telby, that a treed man oughtn't to be sawin' limbs off the oak that's aholdin' him."

It was true that Jake had been baiting Telby all night, losing steadily so he would grow more confident. And more stupid. So it appeared his strategy was working.

It had been a long evening, and Ellie had been squirming in her seat for the past hour, wincing with each successive loss. Now, she was jiggling her leg up and down as if she was riding a poorly gated horse. At Telby's jibe, she shot to her feet through the blue cloud of smoke at the table.

"Maybe he's right, Jake. Maybe I should go back to the—"

"Sit," he snapped, pinning her with a look.

"Right." She dropped back down to her seat, but she didn't like it. She started in on chewing another nail. A barmaid came to refill his glass and he ordered one for Ellie. He didn't like the way the men in the room looked at her in that red dress or the hunger in their eyes. Twice already he'd had to restrain himself from laying a fellow flat with his fist for the way he was ogling her.

He had to get his head back in the game, but sending her off on her own was not an option.

They played out the hand. One by one the others

folded. Besides Raymond, two other men, Tom Calder and Witford Kirby, had already folded their cards but were watching the exchange with interest. Nicholas Telby—the man who'd hired Millie and beaten Leanne last night—sat beside Tom.

He'd spent the past few hours with his eye on Jake like a man with a secret that amused him. Telby was the worst kind of player. His bets were wild and ill conceived, and he would not shut up. His tells were simple. When he bluffed, he picked the edge of his cards with his fingernail. When he had something, he leaned back in his chair with his bourbon. And with each successive bourbon, his voice got slightly louder and his stack of chips, smaller. A man like that could always be led by the nose of his own arrogance. And Jake was just the man to do it.

A fine sheen of sweat had popped out on Telby's forehead as he glanced at his cards, then at Jake to see what he'd do. Telby was already in for two thousand, with six hundred in front of him. He leaned back, sipping his whiskey, but kept his fingers on his cards.

Jake smiled. He'd counted. He knew exactly what Telby had in his hand. And there was no way the man would beat him. "All in," he said, pushing in the last of his chips, some eight hundred dollars, into a pot that had grown quite rich.

Ellie, who had just gotten her shot of whiskey, downed it in one gulp. Her eyes bulged for a moment, threatening to make him laugh. He resisted the temptation and stared at his hand.

If Jake had figured Telby correctly, by now he'd be

comfortable enough with Jake's losing streak to play right into his plan. Sure enough, Telby asked, "How much he in with?"

"That's eight to you," the dealer told him.

Telby recounted his chips, seemingly like a man who'd just lost his dog. "I'm a bit short. Can I get some more credit?"

"No, sir. You're fresh out of credit," the dealer stated.

"But I got two thousand in that pot already."

"That, my good man, is why they call it gambling," Raymond intoned, sending a thick ring of smoke up into the air.

Ellie coughed.

"He does have a point, though," Jake said evenly. "He is in for a fair amount. Surely he's in possession of something…some title, or trinket that could make up the difference? A piece of land, a fine animal, perhaps, or maybe even…a gold watch."

Telby reacted predictably, only just then apparently realizing it'd been Jake's target all along. Jake studied the emotions flitting across his expression like the thunderstorm still beating the river outside.

"Got a horse and saddle in St. Louis. Worth every penny of two hundred dollars."

"I ain't never met a horse worth that," the dealer said. "Got papers?"

Telby shook his head.

"Perhaps you should search your pockets again," Jake suggested. "Because I would accept a gold watch as sufficient trade. This bein' strictly between you and me now."

Telby glanced around the table at the faces of the

men who'd taken a fresh interest in what Jake *wasn't* saying. He stared at his cards lying facedown on the table. His only real question was would Jake expose his thievery?

After a short wrestle with his precarious financial status, Telby withdrew Jake's watch from his pocket and threw it on the pile. "Take it, then."

Across the way, Ellie's knee even stopped bouncing.

"It'll do," Jake told the dealer after examining it.

The noise in the casino grew tellingly quiet as tension spiraled between himself and Telby. Cautiously, Jake withdrew the derringer from the holster on his leg and pointed it under the table at Telby.

"Call," Telby demanded, and laid his cards down. Three kings.

Ellie, perched on the edge of her seat, chewing madly on a fingernail, stared at Jake. He laid his hand down. Three queens, two aces. A full house.

Telby's mouth quivered with fury, but he stood up and left the table without a word. He'd been played and he knew it. And he wouldn't forget it.

"Game goes to Mr. Gannon," the dealer announced. "That moves you to the next round tomorrow morning, sir."

Jake replaced his gun and stacked the chips neatly before him.

"Shall I put your money in the safe again, Mr. Gannon?" the dealer asked quietly.

Jake relaxed in his chair, watching Ellie over the rim of his glass of whiskey. "No. I'll take the cash."

"Very good, sir."

Ellie now stood at his elbow. "That was brilliant," she whispered in his ear.

Her breath, intimate against his skin, stole his air. He caught her hand as it skimmed his collarbone. "Hungry?"

A dazzling smile spread across her face. "Starved."

LATER, THEY SAT at a small table covered in checker-board cloth in the steamer's restaurant. Jake nursed another whiskey and Ellie ordered French claret. Between them, the largest hunk of beef she'd ever seen in her life.

She held the bottle up next to her face like a com-mercial. "Mmm-mm, 1872. A *very* good year."

He didn't get it and Ellie smiled. "It was a joke. Never mind. I used to do commercials. On TV."

"TV?" He looked at her blankly.

"It's a box that people watch with…" She sighed. "You're right. Who cares? I don't miss it. I thought I would, you know?" She suddenly admitted it was true. Jake was endlessly more fascinating than anything pass-ing for drama on television. As she sat across from him, watching him eat, she could feel the memory of him like a palm print on her skin. That sweet slide of his mouth against her throat, his fingers touching her breasts, making her nipples turn into tight little buds. His scent brushing against her like a hot breeze. Even as she sat primly eating her food, the very idea of him made a flush of heat rush to her face. She wanted him to touch her again.

But that was wrong.

Still, she wanted him to. In a way she had never, ever wanted from Dane.

"What *do* you miss? From…" he asked, cutting into her fantasy. "You know."

She thought for a minute as she cut a bite of steak, listening to the backing and filling of the steamer as it made its way up the river. "Lip gloss. I dearly miss that. A hot shower. A direct flight to North Dakota. My camera."

"You're a photographer?"

She nodded. "People, mostly. Faces interest me." She sat back. "Yours, for instance."

He gazed at her through half-lidded eyes. "Why's that?"

"Well," she reflected thoughtfully, "for one thing, it's your cheekbones. They're high. And that shadow they create above your jaw? Well, it gives your jawline depth. Strength. And…your mouth," she went on, "how it quirks up at the corners. But it's really your eyes that fascinate me."

"My eyes?" A small smile of pleasure curled his mouth.

"There's a tiny green speck in one of them. Like a fine splinter of emerald."

He actually blushed. "No, there isn't."

"Yes, it's right there. You never looked close?"

He just smiled again.

"But it's not just the color," she clarified. "It's the secrets you keep there. You can hide from people, but the camera? The camera catches everything."

His smile faded and he forked another bite of steak. "I'm a simple man, Ellie. My secrets are not all that interesting."

She leaned forward. "I think you're anything but simple, Jake."

He drank a little more, watching her over his glass again. "What about you? What would the camera see if it took your picture?"

Ellie sat back, thinking for a minute. "That's a question only the camera could answer, isn't it? I don't see myself as others do. I just see Ellie."

"If I was that camera," he speculated, rubbing his thumb over the rim of his glass, "I'd see a beautiful woman who didn't know her own worth. A woman who can talk her way out of almost anything. A woman who hasn't been touched near enough."

That took her breath away. He was closer to the mark than he could ever know. She stared at her hands, then looked up. "You would see all that?"

He nodded, focusing on her as if there wasn't another person in the room. "But then, I'm not a camera. I'm just a two-bit gambler."

She smiled. "I really know nothing about you, do I? Is it like that for everyone with you, or is it just me?"

"Just you," he teased.

"Mmm. I feel special. It's getting late," she said. "And the wine is going to my head."

He sipped the last of his drink and stood. He went to pull her chair out for her, but she beat him to the punch. Then she felt embarrassed that she had. Jake might be a gambler and a bad boy bent on trouble, but he still had manners, something about which twenty-first-century men could take a lesson.

Jake opened the door to the deck and they walked out into the moonlight. It spilled over the slow-moving river like liquid silver. She wished she had a camera right now to capture this moment. Even in black-and-white, it would be remarkable on film.

She realized it had been minutes…*hours* even since she'd worried about Reese. But the thought of her now did what it always did: sent a rush of guilt through her. How could she be standing here under the stars enjoying Jake's company when her sister was God-knew-where, suffering God-knew-what fate? It was wrong.

Wrong, wrong, wrong.

As they walked along the deck, someone stepped out of the shadows, a lit cigarette dangling from his mouth. Jake shoved her behind him as Telby moved into the spill of moonlight. He was obviously drunk, weaving his way toward them. He must have been waiting for them here since the end of the game.

"Ah, there he is with his lucky charm!" His words were slurred by alcohol and anger. "But she's the luckless one, isn't she, my friend? You took your damned sweet time."

"Get out of our way, Telby. I have no truck with you. You lost fair and square. Good night to you."

"Did I? Or did ya play me for a fool?"

"What you are is no concern of mine."

Telby's hand appeared with a pistol in it. It flashed a dull gunmetal gray in the dim light. "I know you, sir. I know you for who you really are. Did you think you could run away and leave that day in Lawrence behind you forever?"

"Shut up. I'm warning you—"

Ellie frowned. What the hell was he talking about?

"You're warnin' me? That's yer only answer?"

Jake's hand was already reaching for the gun he kept in the back waistband of his trousers. "Put the gun away, Telby. Be glad I didn't expose you for the thief you are."

"You swartwouter!" he strangled out, staggering sideways. "I should drop you where you stand and save them the trouble."

"You're drunk. Go, sleep it off. C'mon, Ellie." He put himself between her and Telby. "He's not going to shoot me."

"What's he talking about, Jake?" she whispered.

"You took everything I have!" Telby shouted.

"You *gave* me everything you had. I did not take it. Now, put that gun away. I don't want to kill you."

Telby laid his thumb across the trigger and cocked the weapon. "*You* don't wanna kill *me?*" His vicious laugh echoed down the deck. "That's a good one, Gannon—or is Gaines the name you—"

But before he could pull the trigger, Jake's pistol appeared, a flash exploding from the muzzle and slamming into the other man's shoulder. Telby cried out and his gun went off wild as he clutched at his shoulder and in a blind rage lunged toward Ellie.

Ellie gasped as he plowed hard into her and sent them both sailing backward over the railing. There was no time to do more than suck in a lungful of air before the icy water closed over her as Telby dragged her down with him toward the bottom of the Mississippi.

8

"ELLIE!" JAKE SCREAMED, frantically searching the black slick of water below for her. Nothing more than a ripple in the water remained where they'd gone in. He didn't think. He simply tossed his pistol away on the deck and plunged in after them.

The freezing water stunned him as it closed over his head, but he shoved up through the surface, sucking air and scanning the surface for her.

Nothing.

"Ellie!" he shouted, panicking. The sucking current of the paddlewheel was drawing him in as he dove under again and fought hard against pull. It was too dark to see anything underwater, but when he surfaced again, they came up, too, struggling with each other in the water.

"Get off me!" she sputtered desperately.

Jake swam the ten feet to where they thrashed in less time than it took to breathe, then Telby took her down again.

Jake dove under and grabbed hold of the man's arm, jerking Ellie free of him and pushing Ellie toward the surface. Telby grabbed his coat, but he kicked him with his boot. He felt the other man lose his grip but find it again seconds later as he climbed his way up Jake's leg.

Still trying to kick away from him, Jake broke the surface and gasped for air. Now he could feel the hard tug of the current as the steamer's wheel drew near. He felt Telby's hand clutch at his leg from below, but Jake kicked him away, toward the oncoming churn of the water. Telby surfaced fractionally, in time to see the wheel approaching, but disappeared in the undertow.

Jake turned his attention to Ellie, who was struggling to stay afloat in the cold water.

"Jake!" she cried. "My dress! I can't—I can't—"

He swiftly dragged her next to him.

"I've got you. Hold on!" He could feel her struggling against the pull of the water and feel her heart slamming against his arm.

He headed for the shore, pulling her behind him as the paddlewheel passed directly over the place where the other man had gone down. He kept focused on the shoreline and watched it come closer, closer. When at last he kicked the river bottom he yanked her toward him and helped her out of the water. The two of them staggered onto the shore and fell, exhausted, across a tumble of smooth rocks, breathing hard.

Jake coughed and rolled to his hands and knees, spitting out water. "Son of a bitch," he spat, shaking the droplets from his hair.

Ellie lay shivering, staring up at the moon, her chest heaving.

"Oh, Jake," she murmured, only now beginning to really feel the cold.

Jake crawled over to her and brushed the hair out of her face. "Jesus, Ellie," he breathed. "Jesus."

Tears had started forming in her eyes. "I thought I was g-gonna die. That would've been just the p-perfect cap on this trip through t-time."

He lay down beside her and curled himself around her to stop them both from shaking. "No chance in hell I was letting that son of a bitch take you."

She started to laugh. She couldn't help it. It just came and came and then it became sobs. He sat up and pulled her into his arms, hugging her tightly against him.

"What? Are you hurt? Talk to me, Ellie—"

"My picture," she said between gasping breaths. "My picture of Reese is gone."

Jake stared out across the water at the fading lights of the *Natchez*. "I'm sorry," he whispered against her wet hair. "I'm so sorry."

His lips brushed her hair, her damp forehead, her spiky wet lashes, and finally, her mouth. She rose up to meet the slashing violence of his kiss with a hunger of her own. His lips were cold, but his tongue was warm against hers, and he drove it into her as if he couldn't taste enough of her. She clung to him, her hands trembling on the soaked, wet fabric of his coat, knowing she should not. Knowing the mistake of it. But knowing this was no ordinary time or place. She only knew this felt as blissful as anything she'd ever done.

Jake abruptly broke the kiss, hugging her to him as if he'd just remembered himself and how much he tried to avoid this very thing. He held her for a minute before he spoke.

"We can't stay here," he said at last. "We've got to get you warm."

IT WAS NO GOOD starting a fire. Jake's matches were as wet as everything else. They were both freezing with cold. Walking was a challenge as they made their way up the sumac-covered slope of the riverbank toward the woodlands beyond. They considered burrowing in last season's fallen leaves for the night beneath the budding oaks and poplars, but Jake urged them on along the muddy track that cut through the woods, sure there would be some destination at the end of it.

He was right. Not thirty minutes later they came upon a small, rustic cabin of daubed mud and logs. Inside the home there was flickering candlelight, and a thin skein of fragrant gray smoke rose from the river-rock chimney. There were two outbuildings: a near empty corn crib and a weathered barn beside a corral housing a pair of oxen and a bay horse, who announced them with a whinny as they stumbled into the yard. The fields surrounding that haven carved out of the woods were plowed and freshly planted.

Jake headed for the door.

She pulled on his arm, still shivering. "But we can't just barge in on them. We're total strangers. C-can't we just…sneak into their b-barn?"

"I'd do as much for them," he said, and knocked.

A young bearded man answered the door with a shotgun in his hands. It wasn't pointed at them; instead, held loosely in warning. He was dressed in grayish long johns and threadbare trousers. He had a kind face, the sort you would ask directions from in the subway, Ellie thought. The man had clear blue eyes, a sandy thatch of hair and a gauntness that hollowed his cheeks. The thin young woman behind him held a fussing baby on her hip whose nose was snotty. Almost as if she and Jake had flipped a switch with their appearance, though, the baby stopped crying and eyed them with apparent astonishment, as if visitors here were as unlikely as talking cows falling from the sky.

"Good Lord," the man murmured at the sodden sight of them.

Blue-lipped and quivering, Jake nodded at him. "My name is Jake Gannon, friend, and…this is my wife. We had an accident in the river," he told them. "We are without fire and would greatly appreciate some place to warm ourselves."

The young man glanced back at his wife, then reached for Jake's hand. "I'm Boone Mayslip. This is my wife, Lindy. Our fire is warm and you're welcome to it. If you've a mind to get out of those wet things, my wife will get you some blankets."

With their clothes drying by the fire, Jake and Ellie sat huddled inside the scratchy wool blankets. As they curved their fingers around steaming mugs of hot turnip-greens soup, Lindy stood behind Boone with her hand on his shoulder. The baby just stared at them with wide blue eyes. "We don't often see folks around these parts, wanderin'," Lindy said. "You gave us a fright."

Ellie tightened the blanket around herself, still chilled

to the bone. "Where I'm from, no one would have answered the door to us. We're very grateful you did."

Jake slid a warning look at her.

"We wouldn'ta turned ya away to freeze," Boone said, as if the alternative was flatly unthinkable. "But we've heard whisperin's of raiders south o' here pesterin' folks about the election. Usin' guns to persuade folks to their way of thinkin' about the vote. Us? We cain't even get into town for such as that with so much to tend to here. You hear any news about it out there?"

"Ohio's governor Hayes is on the ticket," Jake informed him.

That drew a disbelieving look from Ellie.

"You don't say?" Boone marveled. "Who would'a figured that?" He politely refrained from asking them about their "accident," instead wondering where they were heading.

"St. Louis," Ellie answered. "How far is that from here?"

"Thirty-five miles. Two days' ride. A good three or four by shoe leather. If you got the money, the rail head is a few hours by wagon."

This was bad news. Ellie flinched, wondering how they would get there, much less catch the *Natchez* before it left the port so she could recover her photo. Beside her, Jake was no doubt wondering the same thing as he stared at the flames dancing in the wide fireplace.

She couldn't help the leap her heart took watching the firelight play across his face. She couldn't stop remembering the look he'd had in his eyes as she went over the railing. She wanted to tuck herself beneath his arm and lay her head on his shoulder. She wanted him to kiss her again and touch her to take away this empty feeling.

Boone talked about the flood that wiped out much of his crop the spring before this one and his desire to put his family aboard the Union Pacific Railroad and take it west as far as the tracks would take them.

"It ain't that we don't love this place," he was saying, lighting a pipe with a lit straw. "It's that the river loves it more." The baby had been sick, he explained, and the dampness here was unhealthy for him.

"San Francisco's a fine place," Ellie offered, "if you want to get out of farming. Or the Willamette Valley in Oregon. Apple orchards grow there like weeds. That's where I'd go. It'll be a major agriculture hub one day."

Jake warned her again with a look.

"What?" she whispered. "I'm just saying…"

Next to the fire, Lindy nursed her baby to sleep without embarrassment and Ellie noted Jake studiously avoid looking that way. Instead, his eyes met hers frequently with a longing and some unspoken question he seemed to be contemplating.

Lindy placed the baby in his cradle near the fire as they put their dry things back on in the near dark of the Mayslips' bedroom, bumping elbows and knees in the tiny space near the bed. Once, he slid the backs of his fingers against the bare skin of her belly and paused. Ellie held her breath, then covered his hand with hers in silent permission. But he removed his touch, and finished dressing.

Boone offered them the soft hay in the barn for the night and handed them a kerosene lantern. They both thanked him profusely and with their blankets in hand, they bade the couple good night.

THEY DIDN'T TALK as they left the cabin. But Jake took her hand and held it as they made their way out in the dark. Inside the barn the hay was indeed soft and fragrant, and piled loose in the lofts on both sides of the structure. They could hear the rustle and soft noises of the oxen shifting nearby. And from somewhere far off, came the howl of a wolf and the reply of a half-dozen others.

Jake tugged the winnings of the poker game from the inside pocket of his coat. "It might just be the second miracle of the night, but somehow my money and I did not part ways in the river." He spread the bills out to dry on the hay beside them. "Lucky they didn't pay me in gold eagles or we'd both be at the bottom of the Mississippi."

"Is there enough there to catch a flight to Deadwood?" she asked with a sigh.

She heard him chuckle softly as he stretched out on the blanket he'd tossed across the hay. "Only if you're acquainted with a very large bird." He blew out the lamp and motioned her down beside him.

"Yeah, that's amusing now," she remarked. "Just wait till we have to actually find a way there."

Several heartbeats passed before he said, "Don't think about that now, Ellie. Come, lie beside me."

Ellie dropped down beside him, so tired she forgot to worry about the ramifications of pressing her face against his shoulder. His strong arms immediately came around her. It just felt so good to be there; to be alive and be held by him.

He threw the other blanket over them and burrowed them deeper into the hay bed. She snuggled closer. For everything that had happened to her in the past day, she couldn't think of anyone she would rather be with right now than him.

"Warm enough?" he asked.

She shivered. "No." He smelled of wood smoke and the cold river. She crossed her knee over his by way of getting warmer. "Did I thank you for saving my life tonight?" she whispered against his chest.

He appeared to think for a moment. "Not properly, no," he mused, his thumb doing circles against her upper arm.

"Well," she said, "that's entirely unacceptable." She splayed her fingers across the taut vee of his abdomen just below his rib cage. That small motion seemed to get the attention of his lower regions. "I should remedy that right now."

"What exactly did you have in mind?"

"Hmm." Her hand slid lower, exploring the dip of his navel and the warmth of his belly. It quivered in response. "A nice note? My old nanny always taught us to—"

His hand caught hers mid-slide and he exhaled a hiss of air. "I have another notion—" he pulled her fingers against his mouth and kissed them "—that might serve to warm us as well."

"Oh?"

He nodded. "First," he began slowly, slipping one finger under the shoulder of her gown. "I take off all your clothes."

She shut her eyes. The train was coming barreling

down the tracks, but she was helpless to stop it. "That seems...well," she managed to say, "counterintuitive."

"Counter *what?*"

She smiled slowly. "Possible."

In reply, Jake pulled her knee up against his erection so there was no mistaking his intention. Then he pulled her fully across him, his hands cupping her bottom. Ellie laughed and opened her eyes. He was holding her now in the fork of his lap, and had settled her directly over his cock.

In the dim lantern light, he dipped his head toward her, brushing his mouth against hers, exploring the seam between her lips. It had been his idea, but now he asked permission.

She opened her mouth to allow him access, savoring the sweet warmth of him and his breath at her cheek. She wrapped her arms around him, curling her fingers into his hair, remembering how close they'd both come tonight to dying. Impossible to imagine this warmth gone, she thought, this strength, these hands that now hungrily explored the curves of her waist and hips. She was grateful. And she wanted him. And nothing else really mattered.

"Ahh, Ellie," he moaned, trailing moist kisses down the length of her throat. "You taste good."

His kisses tingled on her skin. Her breathing came ragged and unsteady as he slid his hand up her bare leg and underneath her skirt.

He swallowed thickly. "Smooth," he said, sounding surprised, as his fingers appreciated the unfamiliar but fine art of waxing. She secretly smiled. He hadn't seen anything yet.

She touched his hand, guiding it upward toward her hips. He paused when he encountered the strip of lacy thong at the top. She was nearly naked under the dress; no corset or any of the wacky underthings he'd given her to wear. Just her lacy black thong and bra. It felt risqué and bold considering where she was.

He slid a finger under the lace at the side of her hip. "This bit of nothing could make a man forget himself."

"That could work," she said softly.

In one quick move he had her on her back, settling himself between her legs, his thick erection hard up against her.

He quickly dispensed with the hooks and eyes on her bodice and pulled it apart at the front only to stare in wonder at her bra.

"This…" he said, kissing the spot just above the lace, "is nice. But—" he pushed it aside, exposing her swollen nipple "—it's in my way. How do I—"

Ellie reached down and undid the front clasp, freeing her breasts. "Better?"

Amazed by the modern mechanics of it, he smiled in the near dark above her. "Fascinating." He cupped her breasts in his hands as if measuring their weight, then dipped his head to lave one nipple with his tongue while torturing the other with the tip of his thumb. It beaded into a hard nub of pleasure. Ellie sighed, feeling exquisite as he pulled the other one into his mouth and sucked hard.

She'd been imagining what this would feel like since

she met him. With his warm mouth on her, it was so much more than she had even hoped.

He lifted his head and began to knead her breast. "I'm not of the opinion that a woman like you is easily got," he whispered against her mouth as he kissed her. "And if you're not wantin' this, tell me now because in another minute or so—"

"Shh," she hushed, wanting him so much it hurt. "I'm a grown woman. I know what I want."

She kissed him as she went for the buttons on the front of his long johns, working them with her fingers until she could slide her palms along the fine hair on his chest. Her fingers traced along his ribs until they met the ridge of his spine and the strong muscles of his back. He rubbed his chest across hers. The friction of his skin against hers filled her with a building ache.

When she saw him, standing in that sheet in his room, she'd had this crazy feeling this would happen. She couldn't explain it. She could feel her other life spinning away from her, out of her grasp. This felt right. Right in a way her other relationships hadn't felt. And if it wasn't, she didn't care. She would abandon herself to him for tonight. And tomorrow would come, all the same.

His mouth explored the soft span of her neck, nipping gently at her skin. "Warming up?" he asked, toying with her jade necklace between his teeth.

"Mmm-hmm," she answered. "You?"

"Oh, yeah." He slid a finger under the top of her thong, slid it down her hips and tossed it into the hay beside them. He dispensed with her skirt the same way, until she lay naked beneath him. He brushed his thumb against the strip of dark auburn hair left from her bikini wax. "You," he murmured, "are a woman full of mysteries."

"Yes, I am," she whispered, dragging her palm up the inside of his thigh until she reached the apex of his legs where his arousal pressed against his trousers with a throbbing heat.

He exhaled sharply and closed his eyes. "Careful, there, darlin'. I want this to last a while."

"I agree." Though she wanted desperately to feel his warm skin against hers. "But these—" she tugged at his clothes "—are in the way. It's your turn."

He complied quickly, shedding his clothes into the hay beside him.

Watching him, Ellie forgot to breathe. He was beautiful. All the masculine hard planes and throbbing parts of him. He looked as ready for her as she was for him. If she'd ever before imagined an actual roll in the hay, her fantasy could never have conjured a man like Jake as her partner; a man who, only hours ago, risked his life for her and now, made her feel as if she was coming apart piece by piece.

With every kiss, every brush of his fingertips, a wave of heat chased away any remaining chill from the river. She wanted him touching her again.

Now.

Inside her, all over, every inch of her.

His gaze fell across her like a steamy wave, but maddeningly, he made no move to touch her. For a heart-stopping moment, she feared he'd reconsidered.

"You must hear it all the time," he said softly.

Confused, she blinked up at him. "What?"

"That you're beautiful."

Her heart stuttered. Men *had* said that before. Many men. But not the way he just had, as if he could somehow see inside her and liked what he saw. That made her *feel* beautiful and more desired than any man had ever made her feel.

She skimmed her hands up the sides of his corded thighs until she could feel him tremble with pleasure. "I was just thinking the same thing about you. Touch me," she begged. "I need you to touch me."

A slow smile lifted his mouth. He lowered himself over her onto his knees. "Where?" he asked, against her ear. Dragging his fingertips along the curve of her breast, his touch pivoted at her nipple, circling it in slow, lazy strokes until the coil of desire inside her tightened. "Here?"

"Ahh, yes." She shifted her hips restlessly against the blanket beneath them, wanting him to cover her, press his hips against hers. She reached for his hand, but he threaded his fingers through hers and pulled her arms up over her head, pinning her there. She met his eyes and a jolt of need rocked through her.

"Here?" he asked, kissing and licking down the length of her arm on his way to other destinations.

Shivers crested along the fault line of his touch, each one burning hotter, and every stroke dispensed with another ounce of her control. He nibbled her neck on the way to her breast, while his fingers skimmed her hip bones, before dipping lower to brush the wetness between her legs.

She could feel her heartbeat. There, against his fingertips. She longed to touch him in return but he kept her hands pinned above her.

"Or here?" he asked, dipping his fingers inside her. His mouth hovered over hers, brushing her lips in a dizzying near-kiss. Ellie reached up and slanted a kiss against his mouth to remove any doubt that his touch was exactly where she wanted it.

She gasped with pleasure as the tiny muscles within her slick heat clenched at his touch. He dragged his finger in and out of her with an exquisite friction until her hips moved involuntarily against his hand.

Dipping down to her breast with his mouth, he sucked hard on her nipple. An equal and reactionary tug centered low in her belly and she moaned at the sensation.

"You like that?"

With his warm thumb circling her clit, she could feel her control spinning away. She was desperate for more. Every fiber of her being screamed for him to be inside her, filling her. "Oh, yes," she breathed, "but I want…I need…"

He let her hands go as his mouth claimed hers again with raw hunger. Ellie wrapped her arms around his neck and pulled him closer, craving the feel of the soft drift of hair on his chest against her breasts.

He pushed her legs apart with his knee, poising himself at her moist entrance. His breath was ragged, like hers, but he held himself back from finishing what they both clearly needed. It seemed he wasn't through teasing her yet.

Ellie's hands traversed his back and the smooth musculature of his hips as he slid himself into her, just enough to taunt her before withdrawing, only to do it again a little deeper the next time. Enough to make her nearly insensible, knowing only that she needed him deeper and deeper still.

Then he pushed up on his elbows, and when she looked up at him, he was watching her, his gaze intent and unrelenting. It only made concentrating on the undulating feeling of his cock moving in and almost out of her more erotic. Over and over, he dragged her up to the edge of some precipice until her whole body was shaking with urgency.

Slowly at first, then picking up the motion of her hips, he thrust harder and deeper until they were no longer two, but one entity, moving together.

Ellie's senses narrowed down to that one point of contact as at last, he tucked his arms around her and she wrapped herself around him. She forgot where she was. She forgot everything except the delicious feel of him inside her and all around her. She climaxed in a crashing orgasm that made her muffle her cry against his bare shoulder.

When he knew she'd finished, he let himself go. Their bodies collided with the force of his thrusts and the sound that escaped him when he came was primal. He shuddered hard into her and then collapsed against her shoulder, murmuring her name.

MINUTES LATER, Jake rolled off her and lay still, listening to Ellie's breathing return to normal. He couldn't seem to get hold of his own. It had been a long time. But it wasn't that. It had never been like *that*. Sex was sex, but that…that was something else. Holding a willing Ellie in his arms had driven every other experience from his mind. She was unique, fetching.

Dangerous.

Now, he understood why allowing himself to get close to her was something he should have avoided at all costs. Because he only wanted more. It was like an addiction. One taste of Ellie and it would never be enough.

Ellie affectionately curled her arm across his chest. "Mmm-mm," she sighed. "I'm warm now."

He tugged the blanket up over them, then laced his fingers through hers, recalling the diamond ring on her hand. "Good," he said, kissing her hair. "We should try to get some sleep. Morning will come fast."

"Jake?" She snuggled against his shoulder.

"Yeah?"

"Thanks for saving my life."

He didn't answer mostly because he feared it might be the other way around.

9

THE NIGHTMARE CAME, as it always did, sneaking in on the heels of a dream that was good. An old nemesis, it found unique ways to lull him into complacency before striking like a coiled copperhead.

Ellie was standing in a river up to her knees, splashing water his way with the flat palm of her hand. She'd been laughing and beckoning to him. Her necklace of jade and gold dazzling in the sun.

But smoke drifted across her, thick with the scent of wood burning and that other smell he could never purge from his memory. Jake turned away from her to find himself fifteen again and on that Lawrence street at dawn, chaos from one end to the other. He waved the smoke away but the acrid odor in the air and the taste of metal in his mouth persisted.

Wake up!

Four hundred raiders crawling over these streets like lice, sucking the life from them. His heart clanged against the wall of his chest as he charged down the street on horseback, that old familiar panic rising up in him.

The raiders galloped from one street to the next, whooping like lunatics and firing guns everywhere, even into open doorways as innocent folks tumbled out into the dawn. Bill Hulse and Joe Maddox took aim at a pair of men cowering in front of a smoking building and cut them down. Bob Younger tore past him on the street beside Fletch Taylor, Besson and Quantrell himself, ferreting out every grown man that lived.

Jake's own six-shooter hung unused at his side. He'd been a damned fool not to have known. Not to have realized what they meant to do in their fervor. Not justice. Murder.

And now it was too late. Too fucking late.

He'd lost track of Sam. Sweat poured into Jake's eyes as he dismounted and, pulling his hat low, walked straight down the middle of the street. The noise and gunfire around him merged into a low, unintelligible hum.

Wake up!

He stepped over the bodies littering his path, and hardened himself to the screams of women abandoning their burning homes. Suddenly, an old man crashed through the window of the nearby mercantile as Sid Creek unloaded a gun into him. Another man ran from a raider who'd taken a bead on him. He rolled to a stop at Jake's feet, red-slick with death. Jake stepped over the man's body as Cole Younger shouted, "Use your pistol, boy," then turned away to find another victim.

Jake kept his gun at his side and continued walking. Bullets whizzed past him, but he was invisible. Probably damned. He didn't know.

From the next doorway he passed, a man appeared with a rifle in his shaking hands, choking on the smoke. A woman cowered beside him as he fired at Jake. Jake braced for the bullet but nothing hit him. The man fired again. And again. And again.

Jake walked toward them and the man kept shooting, but it was as if he was a ghost. A ghost of himself. He watched the horror creep into the man's expression as he ran out of bullets. Jake ripped the empty rifle from his hands and hollered, "Take those horses," pointing at the pair of white-eyed mounts panicking at a nearby hitching rail. "Go! Run!"

The couple sprinted for the horses, but seconds later Frank James dropped the man like a stone, then whooped like a banshee. To Jake, he said, "Thanks, kid. We make a good team. Like pickin' quails off bushes, ain't it?"

Frank wheeled his horse around and tore off in search of more murder. Jake aimed his gun at Frank's back and fired, but his shot pulled wide. Just beyond Frank, a townsman making a run for it caught the bullet instead. He fell sideways into the dirt and never moved again.

Jake heard himself scream and made to run. But his feet were rooted to the spot as if he were knee deep in muck. He couldn't move, no matter how he tried. And the fire was coming for him. Higher. Higher, it arched over him like a giant hand to pummel him down. He screamed again as—

"Wake up, Jake!"

—the fire seared up his back and—

"Jake!"

He blinked, disoriented, his chest heaving and the darkness around him pressing in. He opened his mouth to speak, but only some unintelligible sound came out.

"Shh, you're dreaming, you're dreaming," Ellie assured him, brushing his hair off his forehead. "You're safe."

He felt as stupid as he'd been then and as vulnerable. He threw a sweaty arm across his eyes, trying to blot out the sight of her leaning over him. It had been years since anyone had caught him in his nightmare. Because he didn't spend nights with anyone but himself. Until her.

"Are you okay?" she asked.

"I'm fine." He was. He would be. He turned over, with his back to her, not wanting her pity. It was humiliating enough.

So she lay down beside him again, without touching him. He knew he'd hurt her, but there was nothing for it. He wasn't about to share that part of his life. Once she knew who he really was, it would be over.

And long after he heard her breathing return to the deep, regular sound of sleep, he lay wondering how it was that some men were lucky enough to have a woman like her for a lifetime. Someone who cared about him, even when he was in the fire.

JAKE WOKE to find Ellie gone, only an indentation in the straw left where she had been. He sat up, rubbing the sleep from his face. Morning burned outside the dark interior of the barn and sprang through the cracks like brilliant strings of light. He peered through one and saw her walking under the trees toward the road they'd followed here. He started to call out for her but thought better of it and put on his clothes.

What had happened between them last night before the dream, and even after, felt unreal. It was like fitting himself into a puzzle that had always eluded him. Like finding where he belonged. That's how he knew it was wrong. Because trusting that kind of sentiment was as dangerous as trusting a man like Luc Besson. And more so for her than for him.

He gathered up his dry money, pulled on his clothes and walked out to meet her at the spring, where she was splashing water on her face. She glanced up as he drew near. Damn, she was pretty.

"Hi."

"Mornin'," he responded. "See you found the spring."

"I could use a bath, but this will have to do. You wouldn't happen to have a toothbrush on you, would you?"

He held his arms wide. "But they probably keep some baking powder inside."

Ellie nodded and splashed some more water on her face.

"About last night," he began.

Ellie looked at him expectantly. "About…what? Us or the nightmare?"

"Both."

"Ah."

"The sex was—" He faltered. "What I'm trying to say is—"

Staring at the spring, she laughed, wiping the water off her face. "Look, if you're going to apologize or give me one of those hackneyed old lines like, 'It was all a big mistake,' you can save your breath. No one forced anyone to do anything last night. I'm a big girl and I can make my own choices. And if you're worried about strings, don't."

"Strings?" He could not see what *strings* had to do with—

"I was no virgin before you, Jake. Where I come from sex is a bit like candy. To be consumed on impulse. What happened between us doesn't mean anything more than what it was. A good time. That's all."

She was the most confounding and complicated woman he'd ever met, he reasoned, and he had no idea how to handle her. Now, unwilling to meet his eyes, she focused her attention on the rocks surrounding the water. He hadn't gotten where he was at the poker tables by missing a "tell" like that. She was lying through her teeth.

"I never said it was a mistake. Even though it may have been for you."

"You're just scared. Because it was so good."

"When I turned away from you last night, it wasn't because of the sex."

"Really? The dream then?"

He glimpsed the morning mist rising up off the Mayslips' fields.

She turned and hugged her knees. "Jake, I need to ask you something. About what happened back on the boat. What Telby said before you shot him. Was he talking about the border raid on Lawrence, Kansas, during the war? About Quantrell's Raiders?"

And like that, the wind left him, he was unable to meet her eyes. He sat down on the grass beside her. "Yes."

"You were…one of them?"

He nodded silently.

"And the nightmare?" she asked quietly. "You called out Quantrell's name in your sleep and other names, too."

He nodded. In all these years he'd never told anyone about Lawrence. Not once. But he did now because what the hell else did he have to lose? It seemed she already knew.

"I was fifteen," he told her. "Searching for something—who knows what now? I'd been on my own on the streets of New Orleans since I was nine, learning a con, my way around a deck of cards, an untended billfold or two. When the war came it swept me up with the rest of the refuse.

"I fell in with Quantrell almost by accident. Running papers between camps. My unit was killed almost to a man and his rebel unit took me in. They weren't official army. They were a splinter army three hundred strong. Quantrell was a persuasive man. He could turn a phrase two ways to Sunday. A born talker. I bought into all his stories of Federal wrongs. Most of us did. He could make wrong appear right. Up look like down. I was young, impressionable."

"And you rode with them into that town?"

He nodded again. "Me and Sam. Your sister's Sam. He was about my age. We became good friends in the weeks before, but we got split up once we hit town."

He told her about the man he'd gunned down. About Frank James and the others he'd murdered. About Besson, the captain who ate his steaks nearly raw and bragged about how many different ways there were to kill a man bloodlessly. About his friend Sam.

"I met Ezra that day, too. I couldn't stomach what was happening. I found horses for them and helped them get out. His father survived that day, no real thanks to me. Somehow Ezra and I ended up friends as a result of it. I always allowed it was mostly out of misplaced gratitude. But I took their friendship, having no family of my own.

"Sam and I, neither one of us had really understood what was going to happen that day. What Quantrell meant to do. We thought he meant to arrest them as traitors to the Southern cause. It was war, after all, and things happened. We'd thought he meant us to only shoot if they resisted. But that wasn't it. The Raiders never meant to leave any grown man alive that day. They slaughtered 'em, one by one, like dogs in the street. A hundred and fifty men executed."

Ellie tried to take his hand, but he wouldn't allow her to comfort him. "You were just a boy."

"I should've known."

"How?"

"I *killed* a man in cold blood."

She wrapped her fingers around his forearm.

"I'm not asking for your sympathy."

"And I'm not giving it. I'm just saying maybe it's time to stop punishing yourself for what you can't change. Maybe it's time to let it go."

The sun, which had begun to break through the fog, cast a hazy light on the long grass near the spring. He plucked at a flower head of seeds and sent them spinning in the air. "Even if I wanted to," he said, "men like

Telby will never let that happen. He knew who I was. And now, so does the man he works for."

"Who did he work for?"

"Luc Besson. He rode with us that day. His call for blood was only second to Quantrell's. But I don't know why he's on my trail."

"Telby called you Gaines. Is that your real name?"

"Not anymore. I changed it after that day."

She nodded, spinning the ring on her fourth finger. "They say you can't change the past…but that's wrong. I mean, look at me. I've already changed things, haven't I? Things that a hundred and something years from now should have been. I met you. We made love. You never would have jumped off that boat if not for me. Already things have changed. And that's just it, Jake. If you let what *was* control what *could be,* then you're losing the possibility of what *might* be."

"Ellie, you know who I am, what I've done. Being with a man like me, that's no kind of life for you, no matter what century I'm in."

"But I should be the one who gets to decide that." She got to her feet, reached down and pulled him up beside her. "So you do believe me, don't you? About where I'm from?"

Standing there in the morning light, she looked like an angel. And who knew? Maybe she was one, he thought. Maybe that explained everything. But traveling through time from the twenty-first century? Maybe she had. Who was he to argue for common sense when he couldn't keep his head straight around her? "I guess I do," he replied, and it wasn't completely a lie.

Relief spread across her face and she wrapped her arms around him. "Thank you."

He went hard at first contact. That she even wanted to touch him after what he'd told her, made him want her all the more.

She smiled against his chest, then stroked him. "Well, all right then."

He might have come right then had he not moved her hand away from him. There was no denying he wanted her here in the tall grass. He ached to be inside her again. He didn't give a damn which century she was from or who had first claim to her, or even about his own sordid past. He also knew that was dangerous thinking.

"Look," he said, "we should agree that this...whatever this is that's happening between us—"

"Sex," she supplied.

"Yeah, that it was good and we both liked it, but keeping it up could be complicated for both of us, especially you."

"Really?" She smiled, catlike, and reached for him again. He wasn't strong enough to resist. "Why for me especially?"

She slipped her hand against his cock through the fabric of his trousers. It jerked at her touch.

"Because," he explained, "because you're...in danger...by association. With me."

"That's odd. I feel especially safe with you."

"Ellie—"

"What?" She ran the backs of her fingers along his erection until he was forced to grab her hand before he embarrassed himself. He glanced back at the house to see the lights were all still out, then took her by the hand and pulled her deeper into the woods.

When they'd run far enough, he pressed her up against a tree and rubbed against her through their clothes. She was breathing hard, laughing, and her eyes were flashing silver at him in the morning light.

There was no talking this time, just a deep-down desire that seemed to possess them both. He ground a kiss into her and she returned it in kind as she fumbled with the buttons on his trousers. She freed him and took him in her hand. That touch nearly undid him. He slid his hand under her skirt. His fingers found her already wet and ready for him, but he couldn't resist dipping into her and feeling her slick warmth there. She gasped as he slid two fingers along her slit and the small swollen bead that gave her pleasure. Her hips jerked against his fingers and her breath came in shaky gasps. She grabbed the tree behind her for support. She threw her head back and started to come in his hand. But he lifted her onto him and thrust into her hard and without mercy. Ellie made a ragged sound and clung to him, clutching his neck and back with frantic motions.

"Oh, yes, Jake…" she cried, "please!"

In and out of her slick little sheath; in and out until he felt her muscles begin to clench around him. Her moans only heightened his raw hunger for her and the uncontrollable rhythm his need demanded. Her soft breasts beat against his chest as she rode him, clung to him. He pressed against her, losing sight of the forest around him. And they came together, cried out together in a shattering climax that left him sated yet wanting more.

He kissed her again and held her by the tree for a minute without speaking, gathering his strength. Then he set her down on her feet.

"I think I'm still coming," Ellie said, breathless. She pushed her dress down and straightened it with her hand, grinning.

"Something takes over me when I'm with you, Ellie," he answered. "Something I can't seem to control."

"Who asked you to?" She ran a playful hand over his crotch, and incredibly his cock responded.

He took her hand away and held it. "Mercy," he begged. "I need time to recover."

"You're right. And besides, they might be wondering by now if we fell back in the river."

After a few moments, they walked, hand in hand, to the Mayslips' home where they could see inside, the family was already up and moving about. They stopped, by silent, mutual consent, before they entered the yard, as if they both wanted to hold on to this instant and not let it go.

"Jake? About St. Louis—"

"I know."

"You know what I'm going to say?"

He'd avoided thinking about it as long as he could. "You need that photograph of your sister."

"It's the only connection I have—not only to her, but to how I got here in the first place. I believe that photo was the key."

Left unsaid was that she meant to find a way back to her own time. That their time together was marked. And why would he imagine it would be any different?

Hell. He'd lived the past fifteen years of his life balanced on a knife's edge and that had suited him fine. One step either way mattered little in the scheme of things. Why should Ellie's appearance in his life change that? No matter what she said about possibility, the truth was she deserved better than a man like him. And the faster she got away from him, the better it would be for both of them.

The thought sent an ache somewhere to the center of him, but he smiled down at her.

"Steamers dock overnight in St. Louis. We'll take the train. It should get us there in time to catch the *Natchez* before it moves on." He pulled some cash from his pocket. "How about we make a contribution toward the future relocation fund of Boone and Lindy Mayslip?"

IT TOOK BOONE two hours to get them to the railhead by wagon. They left the farmer at the depot counting his sudden windfall gratefully. They'd been lucky to stumble onto the Mayslips. Luckier still that Jake had taken his winnings the night before at the casino.

After a two-hour wait they caught a train to the city. Ellie stared out the window at the lonesome landscape, marveling at how the countryside looked without twenty-first-century civilization. The low rolling hills stretched out around them with untapped potential. Beautiful and stark.

When they made their way into St. Louis, Ellie couldn't stop staring at the place. It looked like a rough-draft version of what a city should be, with short, wood-framed buildings laid out in a neat grid of streets.

Spider-webbing these streets was a network of horse-drawn cable cars jammed with passengers going in every direction. Jake, who seemed familiar with the St. Louis trolleys, hopped onto one near the depot and pulled her up with him.

"Where are we going?" she asked.

Without meeting her eyes, he replied, "To buy a gun. And you need something to wear that's not covered in mud."

"But—"

"Ellie," he interrupted. "Look at us."

She took a moment to do so.

And discovered he was absolutely right. They were a sight, still wearing the remnants of their sojourn in the muddy Mississippi. She wasn't the only one looking, either. Half a dozen of the trolley's passengers were taking a gander at them, too. No doubt wondering if mud was the new fashion statement. And Jake was sporting day-old stubble.

She moved circumspectly closer. "You might have a point."

"*Thank* you."

There were mercantile shops and dry goods, feed and grain stores and a myriad of saloons and restaurants. They made their way to a gun shop where he purchased a small revolver that fit neatly in his boot and some ammunition. At a shop up the street, he found himself a new suit and her a long-sleeved, everyday gray silk dress hanging in a tailor's shop window that had been ordered, but left behind. Jake bought it for her and she put it on, discarding the mess of red silk that had once been clean. The gray one had two pluses: one, it fit her and hadn't yet been hemmed, so it brushed the floor, and two, it didn't look as if she should be standing in a koochie lineup at a nineteenth-century brothel.

Jake left Ellie at the shop as the dressmaker did some last-minute alterations to her gown. He made a quick stop at a bath house and got himself a shower. By the time he'd finished and returned to the mercantile, Ellie was ready.

He tugged her along again as he hopped on another trolley, this time heading to the docks. Half the passengers seemed to be immigrants—Irish, German and Chinese mostly—and the cacophony of languages she heard might just as well have been on any street in modern-day Los Angeles. St. Louis was a real, bustling town with pedestrians fighting their way through a jam of wagons and along mud-rutted streets.

The crowded docks were a vast field of sun-bleached livestock, goods and people waiting for loading onto one of the dozens of steamers at the port. Miraculously, the *Natchez* was still there, loading cargo and passengers onto its decks.

"There it is," she said. "You stay here. I'll go."

"Hell, no," Jake warned, tugging her back. "I'll go."

"But what if Besson is here looking for you?"

"He would've come and gone already and seen I'm not onboard. He's busy trying to figure out what happened to Telby right about now. I'll just get on and get off. You stay here. Every man on that boat knows you by now and they've probably put two and two together about Telby. If anybody's gonna get in the middle of that, it'll be me."

"That's not right. It's my photograph. You shouldn't have to go—"

"You want to find your sister or don't you?" He gave the docks a quick scan. "Just do as I ask." Checking the load on his gun, he tucked it into the strap inside his boot. "You wait right here," he told her, handing her two hundred dollars in cash.

"Jake—"

"Stay out of sight. If something should happen to me, get the hell out of here."

"What?"

"Take this money and get on the first train north toward the Dakota Territory. Find someplace quiet to settle until things calm down. Then go and find your sister."

"Maybe we should just go to the authorities, tell them what happened. It was self-defense with Telby—"

He dropped a silencing kiss on her mouth and said, "For once in your life don't argue." He headed toward the docks.

"Jake!"

He turned to face her with a look that almost broke her heart. "What?"

"Watch your back."

He smiled, then headed off and she watched until he disappeared into the crowd there. She ducked behind a wagon to watch.

The afternoon's steamy heat beat down on her as she waited for him to appear onboard the *Natchez*. Ellie studied the busy docks and the crowds and the confusion. The insanity of her situation struck her again. Here she was, hiding behind a wagon in the nineteenth century, waiting for a man she barely knew, but with whom she'd made love just last night.

He was absolutely the exact kind of man she'd sworn off forever: reckless, impulsive…undoubtedly damaged. How was it possible that she'd started to fall for him already? Even though she knew, *she knew* how it would all end. What was wrong with her, anyway?

Somewhere, a hundred and thirty years from now, safe, financially secure Dane waited for her, was probably searching for her, out of his head with worry. So why did that seem to matter so little to her right now? Did that make her a horrible person? Maybe it was about time she started being honest about her feelings for Dane.

Because it was Jake's kisses and not Dane's that kept shivering through her memory. And what was with the crazy idea that had crept into her consciousness somewhere around 5:00 a.m. that she could somehow, possibly take Jake with her to the twenty-first century whenever she figured out how the hell to get there? But even if she could, and he could—would he even want to go with her?

Which brought her around to the hundredth repetition of the question that had been popping up every few minutes since she'd arrived in the nineteenth century. How would she ever figure out how to get home? She wasn't fool enough to believe that her odds were good that the window, once opened, would ever appear to her again. Time travel was theoretically possible; even scientists believed that. But if she and Reese had both done it, then others must have, too. What if she was only one of thousands…all those people who disappeared without a trace. Maybe they were here or in another century.

All of these thoughts tumbled through her as she stood waiting for the man at the center of them to return. She rubbed her arms, suddenly, for no reason, cold. That's when she looked behind her and saw him. It was none other than that man from Dane's Hollywood premiere, watching her from under the shade of a portico across the street. The second she made eye contact, though, he melted into the crowd, carrying a box camera and tripod on his shoulder.

No. That's impossible.

Ellie shoved away from the wagon and ran halfway across the street, trying to catch sight of him. But he and his camera were gone. She glanced back at the boat. Still no sign of Jake.

Had she imagined it was him? Conjured up a familiar face? Was she going crazy?

Then she spotted Jake moving along the rail, searching the shore for her.

She was about to raise her arm to wave to him when two men stepped up behind him and one of them hit Jake over the head with the heavy end of a walking stick!

Ellie gasped.

Jake's knees buckled, but the two men shouldered his arms to make it seem as if he was just drunk and dragged him down the gangplank between them.

One of them had to be Besson. Jake had been wrong. He had waited, after all, sure he'd come back to the *Natchez*.

Oh, no, this was all her fault! She tried to think what to do as she pushed her way through the crowded dock toward them. But at the end of the gangplank, they shoved him into a covered carriage and took off, whipping the horses down the crude dirt road that paralleled the river.

"Stop them!" she shouted. "Someone stop that carriage!"

Several men noticed her, but no one could have done anything to stop them at that point.

Ellie could only stare at the bastards who had Jake as they disappeared behind a cloud of dust.

10

WHERE THE HELL was Google when you needed it? The yellow pages? The freakin' FBI?

Ellie had so never fully appreciated the twenty-first century until now, when she needed it most, and here she was stuck in the damn Dark Ages!

She stumbled on a muddy rut as she crossed what was generously called a street. She cursed and hopped on one foot, readjusting her strappy high-heeled sandal—the sandal that was well on its way to falling apart after its erstwhile dip in the muddy Mississippi and three hours of traipsing up and down these horrible streets looking for the only person who might be able to help her find Jake.

"I'm looking for a man named Ezra Kane," she told the man mixing remedies behind the counter at the druggist shop. "Do you know him? He's a photographer. This tall, a goatee…"

It was at least the hundredth inquiry she'd made about him and the response here was no different.

The druggist shook his head. "No, ma'am. Can't say I know him. Try over on Sixth. Horace Ebell's got a photography studio. Reckon he might know."

But she'd already been up and down Sixth Street and asked at that shop with no results. She thanked him and left the store, heading back out to the lowering sky that looked like rain.

In the hours she'd been prowling St. Louis, she'd formulated and discarded several plans to try to save Jake. Going to the sheriff was no good. It would only get him into more trouble.

Besides, why would the police help her? Dozens of men must have actually witnessed Besson dragging Jake off in that wagon, and not one of them lifted a finger to help him. She reminded herself that she was not in Kansas anymore. Or in L.A. She was in the Wild West and things only worked according to the rule of law here when it suited the people in charge of the rule of law. Her choices narrowed down to one.

The photographer.

Somewhere between the docks and the end of the Fourth Street commerce district, it hit her who he was. At least, she was almost certain. But why would Ezra Kane, Jake's supposed friend, walk away from the docks like he did? Why would he hide from her?

Oh, he had been watching. In fact, he'd been expecting them. She had no doubt of that. So why the mystery? And where the hell was he?

She had the strangest feeling he had somehow orchestrated this crazy detour in her life. He was the one who had sent her back to the attic. The one who'd told her time was running out. In the future, of course, where he had *also* traveled through time. It all made sense now. The whiskers, the windowpane checked suit that looked like a theater department castoff. Half the men on this street wore suits just like that one. Ezra Kane had traveled through time to get to her and now he had simply abandoned her here.

Why?

As cosmic mistakes went, this one was turning out to be a doozy. Exhausted and on the brink of panic, Ellie climbed on a crowded trolley, paid the driver the nickel fare before collapsing on a hard bench seat. She felt close to tears and did her best not to imagine what was happening to Jake right now. Besson wasn't beyond murder. Jake had said as much. Three hours had passed. For all she knew he could be—

A sound drew her attention across the crowded car. There, sitting on the bench seat across from her— behind the blond boy with the cute straw hat standing beside his father—sat the object of her search.

"Holy crapola!" Ellie shot to her feet. "You!"

Ezra Kane was already watching her and stood, making a conciliatory gesture with his hands. "Calm down, Miss Winslow—"

"Calm down? Calm down?" she practically shrieked, drawing shocked stares from the people around her. "Are you *kidding* me?" She pushed past the man and his son. "Where the hell have you been, you freak? You did this to me, didn't you? You brought me here and then you just ditched me!"

He had the nerve to wince. "It's more complicated than—"

Yanking him toward the exit, she lowered her voice to a strangled whisper because by now she had the full and somewhat alarmed attention of everyone on the car. "*Complicated?* I'll give you complicated. Somebody's taken my friend, Jake Gannon, and right now, they may be hurting him. *Very. Badly.* What do you say to *that,* Mister Fast-and-Loose-with-the-Centuries Kane?"

He reached up and pulled a cord that signaled to the driver. The trolley rolled to a stop at the next corner and the two of them leaped out.

The trolley pulled away and she pinned Ezra with a furious look. "Talk. Explain yourself. Go on. I really want to hear this."

"We should go somewhere more pri—"

"How about the twenty-first century, huh? How about that?"

He frowned at her, then glanced uneasily around them at the people passing by, hiking up the collar of his brown tweed jacket. "Is that what you want?"

"Why? Are you the man behind the curtain? Should I click the heels of my ruby slippers together three times and say there's no place like home?"

"Is that what you want, Miss Winslow?" he repeated.

Yes! Wait, no... Oh, damn him! "That's a trick question. Of course I want to go back. But first I want to save Jake and you know it. This is all your doing."

"I confess, I brought you here, yes," he said, guiding her off the street toward a nearby walkway. "But it was because he needed you."

"Needed me? Who? Jake?"

"Yes."

He hurried her down the walkway, but she had no idea where they were going. "What the hell does that mean?

He was perfectly fine before *I* interfered with his life. And I thought I came back here to save Reese. *Didn't I?*"

He didn't reply. He just kept on walking.

"I suppose you brought her back here, too."

He ran an uneasy hand over his goatee. "That's right."

"Look. We've got big problems. Jake is—"

"I know all about Luc Besson and what happened at the docks."

She gaped at him. Several awful seconds slid by. Then anger rose up in her like a flash of heat. She so wanted to haul off and slap him. Hard.

"Wait," Ezra said, taking in her expression. "I left before they took him, but by the time I got home, there was a note nailed to my door telling me where to meet if I wanted to save Jake's life. I've been looking for you ever since."

She shook her head, not understanding. "If it's between you and Besson, then why take Jake?"

Ezra swallowed hard. "Because Besson is using him to get to me. He knows I won't let him kill Jake."

At his words, the sidewalk began to spin and she swayed on her feet.

Ezra steadied her with a hand under her arm. "How long since you ate something?"

She couldn't remember. She was light-headed with fear. "No, we have to find Jake—"

"Besson said sundown. That's another hour away. Come with me. You are no good to anyone half-starved."

COLD WATER HIT JAKE hard across the face.

He gasped, opening his eyes to the dim light of an

unfamiliar place and the blurry image of a man standing beside him. His shoulders burned, his arms felt as if they were being pulled from their sockets. He looked up to find he was suspended by his wrists from a rope.

"Hello, Jackson," the man said. "I knew I'd find you one day."

Jake squeezed his eyes shut against the pain at the back of his head, feeling his senses return, one by one. His hands were numb, his head ached and something sticky had dried down the back of his neck. The scent of a hay-filled loft drifted down from above and the ripe scent of horse dung came from a handful of stalls filled with the beasts watching them over the rails of their enclosures.

"I do apologize for the use of my cane," said the man nearby. "How is your head?"

Jake cracked an eye, then shut it again. "What the hell do you care, Besson?"

That seemed to please him. "You remember me."

"The way a man remembers a festering wound."

Jake thought the room was spinning a bit, and he braced himself against the floor to make it stop. Besson circled around him observing him from all angles, only adding to the dizzying effect. Thirteen years had been unkind to the man. He wore it hard around the eyes and mouth, and his hair had gone entirely gray. He limped, using a burled-maple cane. He had Jake's watch in his hand and he was flipping the engraved cover open and closed. Lying on a table nearby was Ellie's picture of her sister, Reese.

Shit.

The metronomic rhythm of the watch cover clicking felt like small explosions in Jake's head. Besson meant to kill him. Of that he had no doubt. Why he was toying with him now was another matter.

"I must admit, finding you did present its challenges," Besson said, taking a seat on a backward-facing chair opposite him. He draped his arms across the spindled back. "But entertaining and well worth the hunt."

"The next time you hire a man to rob me, send someone better. Your man's eating mud at the bottom of the Mississippi."

"Is he?" Besson asked, as Telby stepped out of the shadows, grinning and rolling up the cuffs of his sleeves. A pair of brass knuckles were on his right fist.

"Thought you finished me, eh, Gannon?" Telby said. "I'm not so easy to kill, am I?"

Besson smiled thinly. "Right now you're probably wondering, 'Why am I here?'"

Jake tried to moisten his lips, but his mouth felt like cotton. "It did cross my mind."

"Well," he allowed, "I could say it was for the reward on that Wanted poster I saw for you in town. Something about card cheating and a New Orleans plantation you stole in a game of faro?"

Jake half smiled. "LaFarge was just mad because after I took everything he owned, I slept with his wife."

Besson chuckled. "Well done. But intriguing as that is, that's not why you're here. I could say it was because of Lamar Watkins. You remember him." Besson checked his gray hair in the shard of mirror hanging incongruously on the post in the middle of the barn.

Against his will, Jake reacted. Watkins had been a

raider with Quantrell as well. A righteous Southerner who believed in the cause, but a bloody murderer all the same.

"Yes, I thought you would," Besson said. "He did hire me, after all, to find you. Something about loose ends fucking up his upcoming political run. Quantrell's debacle is an untidy bit of business for all of us, isn't it? Anyway, while it's partly true that Watkins is the reason you're here, that would not be entirely accurate."

"Be accurate then."

"Fair enough. A worm on a hook is what you are, my young deserter, nothing more."

He liked the direction of this even less. "Bait? For what?"

The man picked up the photograph of Reese and ran his finger across the woman's face. "Beautiful. And if I'm not mistaken, the man beside her is young Sam Keegan. Your friend, no? He's next on my list."

Jake watched him through lowered lashes, wanting to kill the man, slowly.

Then, Besson turned the picture over. Looked at Ezra's stamp.

"But," Besson continued, "they interest me less than this man and what he can do."

AT A CAFE Ezra ordered her the fastest thing on the menu: steak and eggs, and strong coffee. After a few sips of the dark brew, her head began to clear.

"I…I'm sorry I yelled at you," she said quietly, holding her warm cup in two hands. "I don't usually lose control like that."

Ezra shrugged. "I had it coming. I'll grant you that."

Ellie ran her finger along the rim of the cup. She couldn't look him in the eye.

"We're going to get him out."

She couldn't stop picturing Jake slumped between the two men who'd taken him. "What does Besson want?"

"This." He patted the case on the chair beside him. "And he's decided there's only one way to get his hands on it. That's to use my friendship with Jake."

"Wh-what is it?"

He studied her for a protracted moment before opening the case and letting her see inside.

The coil of fear that she felt tightened another notch. It was a box camera—exactly like the one she'd found in the attic. "Is that what I think it is?"

He nodded. "It's how I *get* from here to there."

It would have been impossible to believe if she hadn't experienced it herself. *It wasn't the picture. The camera was the device. The time-travel machine.*

Oh, hell, that sounded semidelusional.

The waiter delivered her food. The steak was still sizzling. She waited until the waiter had left them alone before she spoke.

"You're telling me that's how I got here? Because of the one I found in the attic?"

He nodded, sipping coffee from his mug. "I'm working on a smaller version, more like the ones in your century. But I have yet to perfect it."

Hope lurched within her. "And…can this one get me back?"

He hesitated before answering. "Yes."

"What about Jake?"

"What about him?"

"Could he go, too?"

Ezra moved his cup to cover the circle of moisture it made on the table. "I'm afraid so far it can only manage one person at a time."

The news twisted the knot even tighter. Ellie stared at her plate of eggs and steak. "And Besson knows you have it? He knows what it is?"

"Yes. And he's tried to steal it a few times. But I've managed to leap before he can get it. He's frustrated. Ambitious. And he wants the power the camera can give him."

"It must have that effect on everyone who owns it," she retorted.

He watched her with those intense blue eyes, probably hoping for sincerity. But he had the kind of face that could go either way. If he'd been five it might have been adorable. On a man of thirty or so, it only made her nervous.

"I only use it for good," he said.

"Ah, is that what you call it? I find it interesting that your definition of good is to destroy the lives of two innocent people by throwing them backward in time." She took a bite of the eggs and couldn't help taking another. She was hungry. But more, she was angry.

"Have I indeed ruined your life, Miss Winslow? I saw you with him. I saw him kiss you on the docks."

"That was private," she insisted, but it was true what he said. How could she claim a ruined life when she'd met Jake here? When she couldn't imagine her life without him now? "What about Reese? Where is she? Is she alive?"

His expression was circumspect. "The last time I saw her, she was in a small town named Hay Camp some forty miles south of Deadwood. She's with Sam. She was fine, Miss Winslow."

"Fine? In a place called *Hay Camp?* In the *nineteenth* century? Obviously you don't know my sister. She's a celebrity physician, she's on TV. She's…well, she's brilliant."

"Perhaps there are things about her that you don't know."

There was something very close-to-the-vest about him. Something she couldn't quite put her finger on. He reminded her of a Hollywood agent she'd once known. "I know that men have tried to conquer time travel for centuries. What makes you so special?"

He smiled, but only slightly. "I'm not the only one. There are many of us."

She blinked at this revelation. "Many?"

"You may already know others without realizing it."

"A secret society?" she asked in a lowered voice.

He chuckled. "In a way, I suppose. Yes."

She sat back in her chair and stared at him. "It goes against all common sense to believe you, but how can I not?"

"Indeed. You're now one of us."

She gulped some more coffee, wishing it was a caramel *macchiato* from Starbucks. Oh, how she missed those things that had once seemed so normal. How she missed normal conversations that didn't involve paranormal phenomenon and revelations that turned everything she knew on its ear. "Why us? Why Reese and me?"

"Because I owed a debt, Miss Winslow, to Jake and to Sam. And you wore the necklace."

She touched the jade necklace at her throat. It had come down through her family for generations, according to Grandma Lily. "But what could that possibly have to do with—"

"It helped me find you. But I cannot…" he began uneasily. "I am not at liberty to explain it to you directly."

Ellie folded her hands beneath her chin. "How convenient for you, Mr. Kane. You stir the trouble, your hapless victims pay the price."

He toyed with his coffee mug without meeting her gaze. "Perhaps," he said, "you will come to find the price fair."

Her life flashed before her, then, the life she'd had once: Dane, her photography, her career as a model; the horrid paparazzi, the red carpets, her crazy parents. And it merged into images of Jake—of him loving her in that barn. Of him winking at her at the poker table as he was "losing" to Telby, and the feel of his strong arms around her as he fished her out of the river.

Was it possible to love someone so quickly? Was it possible that Ezra might be right about her destiny?

But none of that meant anything if they couldn't save Jake now. Ellie pushed her plate of food away from her and pressed her palms on the table, trying to calm herself down. "So, Mr. Kane, you must have a plan, right? To rescue him?"

"And I have a plan to keep you out of harm's way."

"Oh, no. I'm not staying behind," she told him.

"Besson is as unpredictable and deadly as a cotton-mouth. He's as likely to kill us as to take what he's after."

Of that, she had no doubt. "Then," she said, "we'll have to bring something to the table that he doesn't expect, won't we?"

11

JAKE OPENED HIS EYES to darkness and the sensation of swinging. He had the vague recollection of Telby beating him, demanding information on what he claimed that camera of Ezra's could do. Move through time, is what he'd said.

The truth cut through him. Dear God. She'd been telling the truth all along. And Ezra was in the middle of it all. But Jake had given Besson nothing. Any piece would only connect him to Ellie. And that he would never do. But if she'd done what he'd told her and gotten on that train out of town, there would be no way to find her. And he prayed she had. But when was the last time she'd done anything he'd said?

The image of her smile sprang up in his mind. Those gray eyes. How she stood toe-to-toe. A twenty-first-century woman. The first good thing to happen to him in a very long time.

Even now, hanging here by his wrists and bloodied, the thought of her stirred something inside him. Not lust exactly…well, yes, lust. But also something much more unfamiliar: a passion to know her. His curiosity about her wasn't near satisfied yet. No, he'd only just begun to scratch the surface. But he would likely never satisfy it now.

Because here he was dangling from a rafter, his past catching up to him again. That, he would never outrun. Even if he survived, did a woman like her deserve a life with a man like him?

Hell. No use asking questions like that now. The more important one was how could he protect her from it now?

His feet barely brushed the floor, enough to support some of his weight if he pushed hard. Damn Besson. He hurt everywhere. The pig was nowhere to be seen.

The horses inside the barn nickered, their breath steamy clouds in the cool evening air. He wondered about Ellie. The last he'd seen her she was standing at the docks watching him. Was she all right? Had Besson found her? Why had Besson left him here alone? He intended to use him against Ezra somehow, but now all he could think about was how to get the hell out of these ropes and put his feet flat on the floor again.

He surveyed his situation. Nothing near enough to stand on or use as a weapon. He peered up into the darkness above him at the rope dangling from the open beam. He curled his fist around the rope tying him and after three tries, slowly inverted his position so he got his foot tucked around the rope above him. That allowed him to slacken the knot around his wrists. Untying it was another matter. He worked at the ropes with numb fingers until he heard the sound of footsteps and voices approaching outside.

Besson.

He jerked his wrists hard one final time, forcing the

rope to give. And then he managed to slide his wrists from the knotted rope. Blood rushed back into his hands. There was no time to escape. He dropped to the floor just as Besson was pulling open the door to the barn, and he slid his wrists back into the loop of rope to make it appear he was still tied.

Besson strode into the barn ahead of Telby. The older man had a smirk on his weathered face as he eyed Jake. "Ah, you're awake. Good. You're just in time to see your friend Ezra meet his maker." He pulled a bandanna from his pocket and proceeded to tie it in a gag around Jake's mouth.

Jake wanted to kill the son of a bitch, but decided he'd wait for his chance. Telby moved to the door with his pistol in his hand. Besson's was tucked into the waistband of his trousers. Jake needed the man to move closer to him.

Telby peered out the door and turned back to them. "He's here."

He?

"Alone?" Besson asked.

"Don't see nobody with him."

"Show him in," Besson said, moving out of Jake's reach. "Let's get started."

Shit.

Ezra walked in the door and saw Jake. The stricken look on his face matched the feeling in Jake's own gut, seeing his old friend here mixed up in this. His fingers tightened around the knotted rope, waiting. *Dammit, Ezra. Couldn't you have just gotten the hell out? Why waste your life on me?*

Ezra was unarmed, carrying a case with him, and he refused to set it down. "Jake? You all right?"

Silently, Jake nodded.

Ezra's eyes betrayed his fury, but his voice was quiet. "So," he said to Besson, "I see you hardly kept your end of the bargain."

"He's alive, isn't he? That's all I promised. I see you brought the camera. Put it down."

"You have, at most, five minutes for this transaction," Ezra told him. "I've sent a friend for the sheriff. They will be here in a matter of minutes. If you decide to kill us, they will have your name and your history, too."

"You are more concerned about that than I," Besson said. "Give me the camera."

Ezra opened the box and held up the camera. It looked like every other tintype camera Jake had seen. He twisted his hands, readying himself to make a move as Besson paced in front of him.

"Let Jake go, then I'll give it to you."

Telby raised his gun to Ezra's head.

"You can kill me," Ezra allowed. "You can kill us both, but then you'll never know how to use the camera."

"I'm not going to kill you. I'm going to kill him," Besson said, pointing his gun at Jake. "And if we only have five minutes, then that's all the time your friend has left on this earth."

"Drop your guns." Ellie's voice came from somewhere behind him.

Oh. No.

Jake jerked around to see her pointing a shotgun at Telby, who placed his weapon on the ground.

Desperate, Besson roared and swung his pistol toward her, but Jake launched himself in the other man's direction and kicked the pistol from his hands. His shot went wild and he fell, the gun just out of reach. Jake jumped him, and the two men wrestled desperately for the pistol.

Ellie ducked behind a post as Besson's shot bit into the wood. Telby dove for his gun and came up shooting in Ellie's direction.

As Jake rolled on the floor, fighting Besson's cast-iron grip on his throat, he caught sight of Ezra with a gun in his hand. He and Telby fired simultaneously at each other.

Jesus, no!

He wanted to scream at her to get out, but couldn't find the air. He groped for the pistol above his head. It was only inches from his fingertips. But he couldn't… quite…reach it.

A weird flash of light filled the barn as Jake's fingers closed on the pistol, but Besson pushed him away.

"I will shoot you dead, so help me God! Let him go!" Ellie was yelling at Besson as she moved closer. Besson had the gun in his hand now and he pointed it at Jake as he shoved off him hard and backed toward the door of the barn.

"You kill me, I kill him."

Ellie walked slowly toward him, the shotgun tucked against her shoulder. Twenty feet separated them now. "If you so much as twitch that finger…"

With one last look at the camera on the floor of the barn, Besson turned and fled.

Ellie lifted the shotgun toward the ceiling and fired,

hoping to scare him enough to keep running, then followed him to the door to make sure he'd gone.

Jake was on his knees, yanking the gag from his mouth. Ellie ran to him.

"Jake! Look what he did to you!"

She touched his face, her cool hands on his skin.

"I thought I told you to get the hell out of town."

"As if…" Ellie shook her head incredulously. "But, Jake…Ezra—"

Jake craned his neck back to the spot where he'd seen Ezra last. He was gone and so was Telby.

"Where did he go?" Jake asked, his voice a croak.

"He…leaped. You know?" She gestured vaguely to the universe. "I don't know where to. And why did he leave the camera behind?"

"*Bloody hell!* Maybe he didn't mean to. Maybe Telby shot him."

"Shh. Let's get out of here. I'm scared Besson will come back."

Jake got to his feet and she steadied him. He stumbled against her.

"Look at you. You're a mess," she said, her eyes sparkling with tears. Wrapping her arms around his bare back for a long moment, she held him close. "And next time I say watch your back, will you please watch your back?"

He dropped his nose against her shoulder and breathed her in. "Yeah. But if I ever find him, I'll have to kill Ezra myself for letting you come with him."

"Letting me? Jake, you know me better than that, don't you?"

He grinned, then winced at the cut on his mouth. "I guess I do." He limped over to the camera and bent down slowly to pick it up. "Was Ezra hurt?"

"I don't know, it happened so fast." Ellie reached down for the case and fitted the camera inside. "How will he get back now?"

Jake shook his head silently. He had no answers for her. Only more questions. But now was not the time. With the shotgun in his hand, he grabbed his shirt and jacket and Ellie's picture of Reese and steered her toward the front door. "Did you bring a horse?"

She nodded.

"Hurry then, let's go."

BESSON HAD STOLEN Jake's money and all they had left was what Jake had given her at the docks. They bought tickets aboard the *Far West,* the last steamer heading to Fort Sully, in the Dakotas. It was headed up the wide Missouri River that forked above St. Louis. If Besson was still alive he'd have to find them. And if he managed to track them here, he'd have to wait for two more days for the next steamer to leave. At least they'd have a head start.

Ellie got Jake to their room and helped him into bed after cleaning up his cuts. His eye was swollen shut and his torso was a mass of black and blue. She could only hope none of his ribs were broken.

As he slept, she held his gun and kept watch out the window for any sign of Besson. As the sky lightened to dawn and the boat pulled away from the dock and left St. Louis behind, she couldn't say she would be sorry

to see it go. This town had meant nothing but trouble
for them. And they'd nearly both lost their lives here.
Ezra was somewhere, lost in time without a way home.
Maybe he was dead. That possibility she didn't want to
fully consider. Ezra had saved Jake's life and probably
hers, as well. Someday she'd find a way to thank him.

Fatigue pulled at her as the sun rose and she climbed
into bed beside Jake. She draped one arm gently around
his warm belly and spooned herself around his back.
She felt his hand reach for hers, caress her arm, then
together they fell into a deep sleep.

JAKE SLEPT for nearly twenty-four hours straight. His
hurting body required it. Ellie simply woke him to eat
and drink. Every now and then, he'd reach for her and
she would curl up in his arms as he slept. Sometimes
he would kiss her hair or cup his hand around her breast.
Sometimes she'd feel him grow hard against her backside as he held her, but she would slip out of his arms
then. It was for him, she told herself. He was in no
shape to love her. But it was something else, too. Something she couldn't find words for yet.

As he slept, she studied the camera Ezra had left
behind.

This was the key to getting back. If only she could
discover its secret. It was a small box camera with its
guillotine lens cover, the push-button trigger, collodion-
coated plates, leather bellows and rear-pull focus. This
one was small, portable and had two gem lenses, which
meant it could take two identical tintypes at the same
time. These photos she'd seen tucked into small frames

that soldiers and wives kept of each other during the long Civil War.

She carefully avoided pushing the trigger. She did not want to accidentally find herself in another century. Even if she did find her way back to the twenty-first, how would she pinpoint where she had left from?

With a coin from her stash, she dismantled the camera one night by lamplight, one screw at a time. She found nothing. No magic button, no secret notes. Nothing to tell her how to follow Ezra back to the future. She was angry at herself for not asking him how it worked before he disappeared. Because without that knowledge, she couldn't help Reese or herself.

Her frustration did neither of them any good now, she decided, putting the pieces of the camera meticulously back together. If there was some magic to this camera, she had no idea what triggered it or how to control it. The consequences of that shivered over her. What if she never found a way back? What if she was stuck here for the rest of her natural life? She'd actually die before she was born!

Ellie looked up to find Jake watching her. She swiped at the moisture on her cheek.

"No luck?"

She shook her head as if she didn't understand his question.

"The camera," he said, his eyes hooded with some emotion she couldn't name. "You took it apart. I assume you were trying to figure out how to get back."

"Mmm. Well…" She got up and put the camera aside. "I was just curious. It seems to be exactly what it is. A tintype gem camera. Portable, simple. Unremarkable."

"Yet Besson was willing to kill both of us for it."

She nodded. "If there's a secret, it's a secret from me." She crawled onto the bed and sat beside him. A few days had passed. The swelling on his eye had gone down and the bruises on his chest were turning a greenish yellow. "You look better."

"Thanks to you." He reached out and touched her hand. Ellie curled her fingers around his.

"I'm the one who should be thanking you. Or apologizing. After all, I dragged you into this whole mess in the first place."

"Nobody drags me anywhere, Visa. Remember that."

She smiled at the name. He hadn't used it since that first night together.

He released her hand and glanced at the dark window. There was something in that gesture, of letting her go, that worried her. But she was having trouble reading him. There was something haunted in his eyes. She guessed what he was thinking about.

"I'm sorry about Ezra, Jake. Maybe he'll be okay. Maybe he's found—"

"Leave it alone." Jake ran a tired hand over his stubbled face.

"But there's a chance—"

"We'll never know what happened to Ezra," he said more sharply than he'd apparently intended, because in the next instant, his face softened. "He may just as well be dead. Just as you are to that fiancé of yours back in your time. Unless you figure out a way to return with that camera. Though talking about it won't change anything."

"You *are* mad at me."

He shook his head. "There's no mad, Ellie. What is *is*. I'm just being clear-eyed, is all. We're, both of us, chasin' our tails here. You lookin' for your sister who's God knows where. Me followin' you. Pulling you into something ugly that happened almost thirteen years ago. It's like we're on a wheel chasin' ourselves. And the only way it can end is…bad."

She bowed her head, trying to think what to say to fix this. He was right about all of it. But she couldn't let herself go there. There had to be answers about Reese, about this camera. And about her and Jake. It was about what Ezra said, about her destiny. And somehow it was intertwined with Jake's. She believed that with all her heart.

She opened a drawer near the bed and pulled out a straight razor. "I bought this for you from a barber onboard. If you want to use it, feel free, although—" she ran her fingers across the edge of his jaw "—I think the beard looks sexy as hell. Why don't you wash up? You'll feel better. I'm going to go get us something to eat."

Staring out the dark window, he nodded.

Ellie walked out on the deck and took a few big gulps of the fresh, night air, pushing down the panic in her chest. A bright slice of moon illuminated the shore where they'd tied up for the night. They were making almost seventy miles a day on the river. It was running high and fast with spring melt, and she'd overheard someone say that spring snags were still buried deep in the river, making this one of the safest times of the year to travel. That was good because the Dakotas were far upriver. That was going to make for a long trip if things stayed this way with Jake.

Somehow, she hadn't been prepared for his anger, though she should have been. He had every right to it with Ezra vanishing and her walking into his life and tossing it upside down.

It didn't matter than she was falling in love with him. Jake wasn't the kind of man who would go there. From what she could gather, he never had. Why had she thought she'd be any different?

Ellie swiped at the corner of her eye. So he wasn't going to fall in love. So he'd never intended on coming along to find Reese. What had given her the right to imagine he would? Because they'd made love? She was a modern woman—she *knew* better.

But apparently, her heart hadn't gotten the memo.

That's great. Just great, Ellie. Fall for the first guy you meet when you leap into a new century. Way to think things through. All your big talk about keeping it simple and unattached…

And then there was Dane.

Ellie stared out at the water. Here was what she knew: she felt nothing. No blip on the heart radar for her fiancé. No tingle. Simply regret and disbelief that she'd once thought what she felt for him was enough. Now she knew it wasn't. Even if she found a way back there, it was over between them. She didn't even think it would come as a big shock to Dane, who had probably settled for her, as well. Because Dane deserved someone who could love him fully, just as she deserved it.

It's like we're on a wheel chasin' ourselves. And the only way it can end is...bad.

Maybe, she thought, heading toward the card room. Maybe he was right. And maybe not. Perhaps what Ezra had said about destiny was more right than wrong. Time would tell.

For now, there was only one way to confront this mood of Jake's and that was head-on.

In the casino, she walked up to the bartender and slapped down a couple of Jake's well-earned poker dollars. "Some hard-boiled eggs and a bottle of whiskey please."

12

ELLIE CLAPPED a bottle of whiskey of questionable origin down on the bedside table and fanned a deck of cards across the bed.

Jake, who had just finished splashing water on his freshly shaven face, looked over the towel at her. "What's this?"

"It's only just occurred to me that I am traveling with a brilliant card player and I have not fully taken advantage of that situation."

"Advantage?" He arched a damp brow.

"That's right. Uh-huh. I can play a little."

"You?"

She leaned back on the bed provocatively. "Does that surprise you?"

His gaze slid over her. She wasn't fooling him for a minute. "Not really. What's your game? Buck the tiger? High-low?"

"I've been known to play a decent five-card draw. But my real specialty is Texas hold'em."

"Texas what?"

"Hold'em. Oh, that's right—" she tsked sadly "—you wouldn't know that one yet. That's from *my* time." She pulled two glasses out of the pocket of her dress and clapped them down beside the whiskey. "I can teach you. I might have a teeny advantage, but you'll catch up. There are strict rules, however, required of this particular game pertaining to, uh, drinking."

"Ahhh?" A smile twitched at his mouth.

"Yes," she said. "The *loser* must take a shot and lose an item of clothing."

Jake tossed the towel across the washstand, his eyes pinned on her breasts. "Interesting. And what about playing for money?"

"Money-schmoney! Well, yes. But it can be played for peanuts, as well. Or whatever's handy. I brought nuts and eggs."

He laughed in spite of himself.

She laughed back, then poured two shots and handed him one. "First shot is a prerequisite. Like Texas hold'em 101."

"Here's to that," he said, clinking his glass with hers.

She tossed her drink back and gave a gasp. "Holy crap!" she croaked, and coughed.

He grinned and tossed his back like it was water. "Maybe the teacher should have tested the whiskey first before making up the rules."

She wrinkled her nose at him in reply. "The *teacher* has everything under control, Mr. Gannon," she said, dealing two hands of cards and shoving a clump of peanuts his way. "Ante up!"

THIRTY MINUTES LATER, Jake had not only mastered her little game of Texas hold'em, he had only lost two hands to her. Now she sat holding her last shot of whiskey staring at her winnings—his string tie and his jacket. Over on his side: her shoes, her earrings, her petticoat and the top half of her dress. So far she'd managed to hang on to the black strip of lace that covered her breasts.

But that wouldn't last long.

Jake stared hard at his cards. If he didn't, he'd have to notice the soft way her breasts moved when she reached for her peanuts. Or the way the lantern light spilled over her ivory skin, turning it to satin. In his dreams he'd reached for that softness a hundred times. But he'd be a fool to do it now. Not now, when he'd already decided this whole mess they'd muddled into was a big mistake. A few kicks to the head will do that.

Either way, he'd gotten hard as a rock when she undid that first shoe from her pretty ankle twenty minutes ago and even the whiskey couldn't help him now.

She tossed her drink back, then studied the shrinking pile of peanuts in front of her.

"Your deal," she said.

He picked up the cards and carefully dealt two hands. "You sure you want to keep playing?"

"Hey, pal, I did not waste good money for my Internet provider each month not to make it pay off someday. Internet poker is not just some flash-in-the-pan learning Web site. It's the real deal. I will beat you. I'm just not getting the cards."

"You'd win if you kept your tell to yourself," he muttered under his breath.

"What was that?"

He didn't look up from his cards. "You twist your ring when you're bluffing. That's how I know."

Stricken, she saw she was doing that right now.

He just grinned and threw in twenty peanuts. Ellie narrowed her eyes at him and folded.

"You fold, you lose," he said.

"Fine." She undid the waistband tie on her skirt and tugged it off. Beneath the skirt, she wore only that little black—what had she called it?—thong?

He suppressed a groan and shifted in his seat.

She sat back down, crossing her smooth, mile-long legs, and leaned back, bracing her arms behind her. By no accident, that posture thrust her full breasts in the air. Her erect nipples peeped up through the fabric, taunting him.

His grin faded as he studied them, marveling at the way that piece of fabric held them up so perky-like. He poured another shot and downed it.

"Fortification," he explained. "And besides, you're gettin' ahead of me."

"One more time?" she asked, cool as the green-scented breeze blowing off the river.

He swallowed thickly. She had nothing left to lose but her unmentionables, her necklace and that ring on her hand. "Your deal."

She dealt them two cards each and picked hers up. She curled her hands in tight fists, pointedly avoided touching her ring, which told him something right there. He was holding two kings. He pushed ten peanuts out.

She pushed ten.

She laid down the flop: a seven of hearts, seven of diamonds and a ten of clubs.

Twenty more peanuts went out on his side.

Ellie studied him over the rim of her cards, which she held under her nose. She pushed out a few more. "Raise you ten."

He met her raise.

A flicker of nervousness flitted across her face as she dealt the river card. King of spades.

She raised him five. He met her bet. He didn't want to be cruel.

The last card went down. Jack of spades.

One last round of betting cleaned out her side of peanuts.

"Let's see what you've got," she said as she laid down her hand. "I have sevens and tens."

He nodded. "Good hand. But not quite good enough." He laid down his cards. "Three kings."

She let out a breathy laugh. "You are good."

"Yes, I am," he said, pulling the peanuts toward him.

She got to her feet, poured herself a half shot and downed it. She hesitated before she reached down and undid the clasp on that miniature corset of hers.

And then he forgot to breathe.

She dropped it on his side of the bed. A slow smile crossed her lips. "Your deal."

Jake swept a hand across the blanket, sending the peanuts and the cards clattering to the floor. He caught her by the arms and pulled her underneath him. When he'd pinned her there against the bed with his weight, he dropped a kiss on her whiskey-sweet mouth, then smiled. "You are a witch. That's what I've decided."

Ellie laughed breathlessly. "I might be. I could have a broomstick stashed somewhere. Or some potion full of bat wings and eye of newt to hold you in my thrall."

She was holding him in something, but he couldn't say what. "That would explain what you do to me, woman."

"Hmm," she murmured, kissing his neck. "My devious plan appears to be working."

His hand found her breast and he played with the tip of her nipple until it sprang to attention in his hand. He replaced his fingers with his mouth and sucked hard on her nipple until she squirmed under him. Ellie undid the buttons on his trousers, found his erection and teased it until he feared he'd come in her hand. And that he didn't want.

So, he spread her legs apart and slid down between them. They'd done this fast before. In a rush of passion. He wanted to take his time here. He wasn't through tasting her.

He tore off that piece of lace from her hips and tossed it on the floor, giving himself full access to what lay beneath.

She smiled up at him. She reminded him of a summer day with those eyes of hers, so clear and shining. He wondered what it would be like to see her that way every day.

But as soon as the thought came, he shut it down. Don't think about that. Only think about this…about the softness of her skin and her sweetness that lingered in his mouth.

Leaving a trail of moisture from her breast down the length of her torso, he marveled at the tautness of her belly and the supple curve of her hip. But it was the apex of her legs that had his attention now and his fingers trailed down past the curls to caress her there.

She plunged her fingers into his hair as he dipped his fingers inside her, kissing her belly, moving downward.

Ellie moaned.

But that wasn't enough. He wanted to feast on her there. He wanted to hear her scream with pleasure.

FOR HER PART Ellie ached to have Jake inside her. She'd spent the evening hoping their foreplay at cards would lead to this. But she gasped as he slid down between her legs, clearly in no rush to finish it. His mouth trailed a path of kisses past her hip bone to the tender part of her upper thigh where he nuzzled her with that smooth, fresh-shaven jaw of his.

He wasn't going to—?

Ohhh, hell, yes, he was!

She felt heat creeping up to her cheeks. She'd always been shy about this kind of thing and, embarrassingly enough, had only tried it once or twice. It made her feel vulnerable and exposed. But something about the way Jake did it made her feel comfortable. Almost relaxed. She let her legs fall open as he tasted her down there, plundering her with his tongue. He seemed to know exactly where to go, exactly what to touch. With quick thrusts and parries, he dazzled her with his skill. Soon he had her clutching the sheets, trying not to cry out.

Oh, don't ever stop because seriously? Someone should bottle this feeling.

He teased her for what felt like hours, pushing her to the brink only to bring her back down again. Until she grabbed his shoulders and begged, "Jake, ohhh, damn you!"

She heard his muffled laugh, but then he slid his fingers inside her and she completely lost it. Her orgasm seemed to go on and on and just when she thought it couldn't get better, he slipped himself inside her. She came again as he thrust hard a handful of times before he shuddered and groaned and collapsed over her.

Ellie's breathing came in perfect unison with his. When he finally moved off her, he brought her with him and tucked her against his still-bruised shoulder.

She lifted her head. "Oh, am I hurting you?"

He shook his head and tightened his arm around her.

She relaxed against him. Content as she'd ever been. She felt like purring.

That, she was certain, was as good as it gets. Nothing like her stopwatch sessions with Dane—the ones she could set her clock by. No, Jake was a tender, generous lover. In another lifetime, she would spend the rest of her days lying beside him just like this. And nothing, neither hell nor high water, would come between them.

Time, on the other hand, was the monkey wrench in the works. Time and fate and a ticking clock.

"You're quiet," he said into the darkness.

"Just languishing in the glow."

He chuckled, then he got quiet for a while. When he

eventually spoke, he did it as he massaged her neck. "What I said before…about it ending bad?"

"Mmm-hmm?"

"I didn't mean because of you."

"Shh," she whispered. "I know that. I don't want to think about what tomorrow will bring. I just want to be here now, with you. That's enough, isn't it?"

He nodded against her hair.

But only time would tell if it was.

THEY DIDN'T TALK about it again. They fell asleep in each other's arms that night and every night aboard the *Far West*. For eight days, they avoided talking about consequences and the dangers of allowing themselves this time. They avoided it, but it hovered like a ghost around the tender edges of every touch. Sometimes they lay in bed just thinking.

Sometimes, when he was playing poker, Ellie would study the camera. She looked at it from all angles, but the puzzle of it eluded her.

Then, on the last night before they reached Fort Sully, that word *puzzle* struck her. What if that's exactly what it was?

Surely Ezra wouldn't have designed it to be so easily solved in case someone stole it from him. He would have had some kind of a lock on it. But when the word *puzzle* came to her, she thought of a box her Grandma Lily had given her once. She'd called it a puzzle box. Inside she'd put ten dollars as a birthday gift. But to get the money, she'd have to figure out how to get it out.

Even her brainiac sister, Reese, had finally given up

trying. And then, Ellie had opened it. It was a simple hidden sliding door blocked by the movements of two other pieces. But the mechanics were elementary once she had them figured out. Easy as one-two-three.

Holding the camera again, she pushed and prodded the walls of the box, the edges and the moldings around them. Finally, one clicked open. Then another. And at last the door she was searching for popped open on a thin, invisible from the outside, hinge.

Inside was a four-inch pencil-shaped ivory dial, circled by rows and rows of seemingly unrelated numbers. Lined up on the bar were the numbers 14517093431118154. Behind that, a tiny computerized motherboard that looked like—in fact, exactly like—it had come straight out of her century.

Ellie gaped at it, a feeling of disbelief washing over her. What did that mean? That Ezra wasn't from the 1800s? That he had somehow come from the future? Or that the time-travel machine itself had?

She grabbed a pen and a bottle of ink from the desk and wrote down the mystifying seventeen-number sequence. She was still staring at it when Jake walked unexpectedly back into the room.

When he saw her with the camera peeled open like a birthday gift he stopped cold, then closed the door, and tossed his wad of cash winnings on the bed. "You got it open, then?"

She should not feel guilty for this. She should *not*.

But she did.

She hadn't wanted him to see her trying to find a way back. The truth was, she wasn't even sure herself how she felt anymore about leaving. But she was compelled, all the same, to look. And now there was no hiding the truth from him.

"There's a secret door inside. See?" She showed him the inner workings, which pulled a frown from him.

"What is that?" he asked, pointing to the computerized inner workings.

"That, my dear Jake, is a computer motherboard. And it does not belong to the nineteenth century any more than—" She stopped short and ate what she'd been about to say.

But he finished it for her. "Any more than you do."

She couldn't bring herself to reply.

"What does that number mean?" he asked.

Ellie shrugged, stumped. "The number of times Ezra has time-traveled? The number of rotations the moon has made since people like him started defying gravity? The number of Hostess Ho-ho's consumed by American teenagers in one year? I just don't know. What do you think?"

He sat down beside her and took the camera from her hands. "Maybe it's not one number. Maybe…it's a bunch of numbers pushed together."

Ellie blinked at it. "Hmm, you might be right."

"Divide it up, and maybe it means something."

Ellie picked up her pen and rewrote the number ten times. Then she started slashing lines between different numbers. She started with dates and time. Then reversed them. 1-4-5 could mean a date or a time, as in January 4, 2005, or the fourteenth hour. As in 2:00 p.m. Or 1:45. There was an 0-9 in the number which could be a year. 5-17-09. May 17, 2009. That made more sense. 2:00 p.m. 5-17-09. That made some kind of weird sense.

And the other numbers… She stared at them for a long time with no luck. A street address? A zip code? A bank account?

Jake, who'd been staring at the numbers, too, said, "Maybe they're navigational numbers, like a riverboat pilot uses to steer the waterway? I think Captain Speary once called them longitude and latitude?"

She studied the numbers again. Of course! It was right there in front of them. They were coordinates. All they were missing were the directional coordinates. But that she could probably figure out. She grabbed his hand. "Jake. You are a genius!"

He actually blushed. "Let's go find a map, then."

They went up to the pilothouse and borrowed the captain's navigational maps. And after trial and error, mixing and matching, they found 34°3N and 118°5W— the exact coordinates for what would someday be Los Angeles, California.

She met Jake's eyes over the map. His were a strange, beautiful mixture of victory and the bittersweet realization that now that she'd gone this far, it was only a matter of time before she left him forever. At least, that's what she thought she saw.

How would she ever explain the growing knot in her belly that tightened whenever she thought of leaving him here? Or of going back to the home she'd known. Likewise, she was aware of the impossibility of staying in this time that didn't belong to her.

THE NEXT DAY THEY REACHED Fort Sully on the south side of the Missouri River. It sat a few miles below the Cheyenne River in the southern Dakota Territory and served as the jumping-off point for all the gold rush miners heading to the Black Hills. The Far West was full of hopeful men who were banding together for the trip to Deadwood, which was at the heart of the main gold strike.

Ellie couldn't help but think of the television series based on the historic settlement. Never in a million years would she have imagined herself here, in the thick of things. But their destination was some forty miles south of Deadwood.

Hay Camp, reputedly a settlement pitched on the shores of Rapid Creek at the base of the Black Hills, had sprung up this year and even the soldiers at the fort were not too familiar with its location. Word was it was founded by some gold miners who'd become disenchanted with the whole standing-in-freezing-water-for-a-thimbleful-of-gold business and decided to build a jumping-off point for those who still had the will.

Plenty of stages were heading west in an all-fired hurry to get to the goldfields. She and Jake joined their ranks.

It took nearly another five days to get there, and by the time they did, Ellie never wanted to look at the rear end of another horse again or see a sagebrush tumble. Her brains were scrambled from the horrible roads, and her backside was begging her to leap from the coach screaming as they pulled into town.

Jake was the first one out, though, carrying the camera case, and he held a hand up for her to step down. Her traitorous legs nearly folded under her.

Jake caught her against him with a grin. "Steady."

It was practically the first time he'd held her since they'd disembarked the *Far West*. And he did so just a moment longer than absolutely necessary before offering her his arm. She took it, wishing he would take her off into some alley and kiss her silly. But he didn't. And somehow, she knew he wouldn't. Because he'd been steadily, surely pulling away from her as the days passed.

Hay Camp wasn't much more than the name implied. It was merely the beginning of a town. The rutted, muddy main street boasted a handful of spanking-new stores. Brennan's Mercantile and Miners' Supply, Allen and Scott's Coopersmith and a wheelwright shop lined up along the wood-planked walkway. The handful of saloons were brimming with customers and goodwill even now in the middle of the day. A barely finished hotel called the Lucky Strike looked as if it had gone up overnight.

But that was just the start. The sound of lumber being sawed and hammered seemed to be everywhere, with new buildings sprouting up as fast as the spring crops of hay on the lush, green fields nearby. A huge, old box elder tree stood at the center of town, at the intersection of two streets, shading the road. And there, in the shade, a herd of sheep lingered around a stone water trough watched over by three young Chinese boys.

Farther down the street, fragrant pens of livestock sat filled with available horses and oxen beside several barns stacked high with hay. The sharp tang of a blacksmith's fire lingered in the air nearby, accompanied by the clang of the smithy's hammer against black iron.

She took in the town with an eye toward finding Reese. It was possible her sister and Sam had moved on, she supposed, staring at the milling crowds on the street. More than possible that a town like this one wouldn't be enough to hold her. But Ellie couldn't bear the thought that this whole trip might have been for naught. Reese had to be here. She simply had to be.

"We should get a room," Jake suggested, as they made their way along the street. "Clean up. Eat."

She turned to him and stopped walking. "I can't. Not yet. I need to search every inch of this place first. I need to see if she's here."

"She'll still be here if we clean up first."

She begged him, with a look, to indulge her. He was hungry and exhausted and so was she, but he didn't argue. Instead, he walked beside her looking for the very thing that would take her away from him. In the past few days, she'd mostly felt alone. They'd made love for the last time on the boat and she missed his touch. If he missed hers, he hid it well because he had spent the coach trip here staring out the window, his thoughts as private as he was. His gaze seemed to constantly drift off when she talked to him, as if he was already considering his next destination, after she was gone.

They'd avoided talking about the future. She'd tried once or twice, but he'd put her off. The close confines of the stage had made it a convenient impossibility. And now, it seemed that avoiding it had mutated into something more calculated. As if avoiding might just make it the issue disappear. She decided she would talk

directly to him about this once they were by themselves in a hotel room. It couldn't go on this way, she
thought, examining each person they passed on the
crowded street.

On the boardwalk, she saw a woman kneeling down
talking to a little girl who was holding her mother's hand.
With a parasol over her shoulder to shade her from the
afternoon sun, Ellie couldn't get a good look at the
kneeling woman. But the little girl was laughing at something the woman said. It was the kind of picture Ellie
would have shot with her Nikon in a heartbeat. A picture
that spoke volumes about the woman and the child.

Wistfully, Ellie wondered if she would ever have a
little girl like that, if she'd ever be a mother. Not for the
first time she considered the fact that she and Jake had
not been using birth control these past few weeks. Her
circlet of pills sat forgotten in a bag in her grandmother's house in 2009.

Foolish, yes. Idiotic? Okay, fine. That, too. But still,
it hadn't been an unconscious choice. No woman from
the twenty-first century *didn't* consider it when having
sex. She'd simply allowed it to be what it would. But
now, with the prospect looming of never seeing him
again, she knew she should have been smarter. She
should have protected herself, not only physically, but
emotionally. Still, if she couldn't keep anything from
this place but a small piece of Jake inside her, then so
be it. Maybe that was her destiny.

The petite woman across the way stood with her
parasol, saying goodbye to the little girl, and swung her
sun shade around behind her.

It took Ellie a dumbfounded moment to realize who she was looking at: the blond hair, the porcelain skin, that unforgettable smile that made everyone turn her way when she walked in a room.

It was her sister, Reese.

13

ELLIE STOOD FROZEN, hardly daring to believe it was Reese. She didn't look scared or in trouble. She didn't even look desperate. She looked…as if she belonged here.

Ellie broke away from Jake and plunged toward her sister, screaming like a banshee. "Reese! Reee-eese!"

Her sister looked up, confused, staring at Ellie but not really recognizing her. As she neared, though, her face lost all its color and she swayed on her feet. "Oh, Ellie," she breathed, just as Ellie collided with her, enfolding her in her arms.

Ellie burst into tears. She clung to her, taking in the solid reality of her. "It's really you! I cannot believe I found you. You're here. Alive. Are you all right? You're not hurt or—"

"No, no. I'm fine. Truly fine." Reese buried her face against her sister's shoulder, crying now, as well. Neither of them spoke for a long moment. At last, Reese managed to choke out, "How did you— Where did you—"

"I got here the same way you did. But I've been looking for you since the day you disappeared."

"Oh, El. So much has happened."

Ellie pushed Reese back to look at her. She was the

same, but…changed. Her short blond hair had grown some and it was tucked behind her ears. Her eyes were still as green. It wasn't just the wardrobe…a simple camel-colored silk dress that made her blond hair look even blonder. It wasn't the parasol that matched it or the delicate crocheted lace wrap around her shoulders—none of which a Beverly Hills label-whore like Reese would have been caught dead in, in her own time. No, it was the look on her face that struck Ellie. She looked…*happy*.

"I can't believe it," Reese whispered, still clutching her sister's hands. "Beautiful Ellie. I never, ever thought I'd ever see you again."

"I know." Wiping the tears from her cheeks, Ellie laughed. "I'm a mess, right? We've just crossed the entire state of South Dakota in a damned stagecoach that would be the perfect villain in a Stephen King novel. But I didn't even want to stop at the hotel first before I came to look for you."

Reese kept touching her. "But how could you possibly know we were here?"

"That's a long story. And… We?"

"Sam and I. We're married, El."

Now Ellie felt like swaying. "What do you mean, *married?*"

Jake arrived at Ellie's side just then, looking uncomfortable. Ellie let go of Reese to grab his arm. "This is my… This is Jake, Reese. He's…he's helped me so much. Jake, this is my sister, Reese Winslow. Reese? Jake Gannon."

"So pleased to meet you, Mr. Gannon," she said, offering her hand.

"Pleasure's mine," he replied, shifting the camera into his other hand and awkwardly shaking hands.

"Reese and Sam," Ellie began, "are married, Jake."

"Well…" Jake smiled for the first time in days. "That's some huckleberry. Congratulations. Where *is* Sam?"

"We run a livery just down the street. I have a small practice next door." Suddenly Reese studied Jake anew. "Wait. Jake…*Gannon?* Sam's old friend?"

Jake nodded. "Yes, ma'am. From a long time ago."

"But how did you two—" Reese's confused gaze seesawed between Ellie and Jake.

"It is a long story," Ellie reiterated. "And I'll tell you everything. But there's time for that. I'm dying to meet Sam."

Reese wiped her eyes. "You're right. There's plenty of time."

JAKE HADN'T SEEN SAM for almost five years, but he looked nearly the same. Tall, dark, lean as a stripling birch. But there was a new lightness to him. An ease he'd never seen before. His face lit up like a candle as he looked up from the mare's hoof he was picking and saw Reese walking toward him, only to cloud over as he noticed Jake. Some private communication passed between Sam and Reese in the moment before they reached him and Sam forced up an easy smile.

Reese ran the last few feet and flung herself happily into his arms.

"Hey, darlin', what's this?" He laughed, watching Jake over her shoulder.

"You'll never believe it, Sam. My sister, Ellie, is here. With your old friend, Jake."

She made the introductions and Sam gave Ellie a hug, then turned to Jake. Pulling a rag from his back pocket, he wiped his hands. "It's good to see you, my friend," he said, offering a handshake. "It's been a long time."

Jake took it and half embraced Sam. "Yes, it has. Congratulations on your marriage."

Sam's eye caught Reese's and they shared a grin. "Thanks. It was an unexpected gift."

Ellie's gaze flickered up to Jake, then away. For his part, he found some pale-colored mustang in the horse pen beyond to study. Because something was rising in his throat—something that seemed intent on constricting his air. Something that made him want to turn around and walk away before the bleed got too bad from the ache at the center of his chest.

"Let's go to our place," Reese said. "I'll fix you something. You're staying with us, of course."

Jake shook his head. "Ellie will. I'll get a room at the Lucky Strike."

"But—" Ellie began.

"I won't turn down some food, though," Jake pressed on. "We're starving, right, Visa?"

Reese laughed. *"Visa?"*

Ellie stared at the ground with a nervous laugh. "Teeny misunderstanding. Did I mention the awful stagecoach station food?"

The two women linked arms and walked up the street, heading for the office where Reese had hung out a shingle.

Jake lingered beside Sam as he put the horse he'd been working on in a stall. He looped the rope over the post behind him and turned to Jake.

"How've you been, Jake?" He took in the remnants of the beating Besson had given him. Jake's eye was still edged with a yellowish-green bruise. "You look a little the worse for wear."

"It's been interesting. I wasn't sure you'd still be here with her, *if* we found you," he said. "Ezra Kane's at the center of this thing." He lifted the box that held the camera. "That and this damned camera. Looks like we can't seem to get rid of each other, huh?"

Sam smiled. "Never wanted to. Still have the nightmares?"

"Some." Though they had subsided considerably since he'd told Ellie about Quantrell. He guessed just telling her his secret shame had loosened up something inside him. "You?"

Sam smiled sadly as they walked into the shade of the tack room. He brushed the dirt off his worn leather chaps and hung up a lead rope. "Not so much anymore. You know Lamar Watkins is running for office in Yankton. Good ol' Captain Watkins? The Butcher of Lawrence?"

"Bastard hired someone to kill me on the river." Jake closed the livery door behind them as they started toward Sam and Reese's place. The breeze carried the scent of the horses and fresh hay on it. It reminded Jake of another time when he and Sam had been in charge of the army horses under Quantrell's command. "I guess we're loose ends Watkins can't afford, runnin' for political office. You should know…he's no doubt after you, too."

"I heard. Wrote a letter to the editor of the Yankton paper a few weeks back. Anonymous. If anyone bothers to look into that man's past, he won't be runnin' for anything but his damned life."

Jake grinned. "You always had a way with words, my friend. You'd better watch your back though."

Sam nodded. "Always. It's good to see you, Jake. Except for that shiner, you look okay."

"And you look…content."

"You saw the reason why," he said, gesturing with a nod in the direction Reese had gone. "A man doesn't get much luckier than finding a woman like Reese. And what about you and Ellie?" He waited for Jake to comment, but when he didn't, Sam went on. "That's quite a ring she's got on her hand."

Jake scowled at a paddock full of horses. "That's from her intended. From her time."

"She's promised to another?"

Jake stared off at the town with its skeletons of wood rising in the distance. "Lock, stock and ring. Regardless what's happened between us, she's never taken it off."

"That doesn't necessarily mean—"

"It's plain enough to me."

Sam narrowed a look at him. "You seem in an all-fired hurry to be rid of her."

If he'd sucker punched him, Sam's words could not have caught him more off guard. "What the hell is that supposed to mean?"

"Not for me to say, but she seemed kind of taken with you. Maybe you're lookin' for excuses to go."

Was he? Or was he simply right? Jake wondered. Was it so wrong to protect himself? To brace himself against that kind of hurt? Hell, she meant to use this damned camera to run a hundred and thirty years away from him. Who could blame him for wanting to avoid that inevitability?

What scared him more was her intention to go back to her time, trusting a strange piece of machinery that nobody knew for sure how to work. He didn't like it. But who was he to try to stop her if she had it in her mind that she had to go?

"Hell," he said finally, "we both know she deserves better than me."

Sam tipped his hat. "That's what I thought. And it's probably still true. But, by God, I'm glad as hell my wife didn't agree. Maybe it's time to put the past to rest, Jake."

A bittersweet laugh erupted from him. "The past, the future…they're all kind of jumbled up these days, aren't they? Nothing's really so clear-cut anymore. What about Reese? She never wanted to go back?"

"I'LL NEVER GO BACK," Reese was saying to Ellie. "Never. Not even if I could. I've found my life here. And Sam. What's there for me in L.A.? More celebrity medicine? Expensive clothes? Fancy cars?"

Ellie couldn't have been more stunned by the turn of events. Reese, married? Living happily in a place called Hay Camp in the Old West? But as she sat beside her sister in her rustic kitchen, she realized how much sense it made. Like Ellie, there had always been something missing for Reese in the twenty-first century. No one looking at her life from the outside would have noticed, but Ellie knew. And seeing her here, now, the transformation was remarkable.

"I guess I never imagined you'd be content here. I mean, no computers, no modern medicine…no Chanel or Dolce & Gabbana."

Reese lifted her arms and twirled around. "That's just it. I don't miss it. Any of it. Well," she admitted, "maybe the Internet. But I'm practicing real medicine here, El. Not that parody of a career I had back there. I can really help these people on the most basic level. The upside is no paparazzi, no film crews—"

"—no makeup?"

Reese laughed. "There *is* that. But it's a small trade-off for what I've found here with Sam. I love him. I *love* him. And he loves me."

Ellie smiled, happy for her. She was downright glowing. At the same time, everything Ellie thought she knew was thrown into question. She'd spent the past couple of weeks desperate to find Reese, to find a way back to her own time. Now all she felt was confusion. About Reese, about Jake and mostly, about herself.

Her sister placed the plates precisely on their hand-woven place mats, watching Ellie.

"And what about Jake? Are you two—?" Her eyes widened meaningfully at the ring.

"This? No. Actually, I was engaged in the future. His name was Dane Raleigh. A financier-slash-producer. We met a few months after you disappeared…when I really needed someone. He sort of saved my life in a parking lot one night. I guess I thought that was a sign from the universe that we were meant for each other. But now I know. He was totally, completely wrong for me."

"And lemme guess. Jake is totally right?"

It was Ellie's turn to laugh, but with irony. "He couldn't be more wrong. Seriously. And more…absolutely right at the same time."

Reese squeezed her shoulder.

"But he's not exactly the settling-down type." Ellie toyed with the cloth napkins Reese had laid out on the table. "He as much as told me so. He's a riverboat gambler. He's like a piece of driftwood. Worn smooth, but better off in the current. He came with me here by default in a way." She felt her eyes well up with moisture. "Sometimes, though, I catch him looking off like he's wondering what's there for him around the next bend in the river."

She told Reese about Telby and the fall in the river, what had happened in St. Louis with Besson, and that she believed she had fallen in love with Jake. But even in the telling, it felt like something was missing. Something important.

"El, have you had a real talk with him?" her sister asked. "Have you told him how you feel?"

"And that would do what? Only make him feel more obligated? I don't want to hold him that way. If he'd had his choice, I feel sure he would have ditched me in St. Louis and found the nearest card game. The only reason he came here was to get away from Besson. But it's my fault really that Ezra disappeared. And I think Jake blames me for that."

"Actually, you don't know what he's thinking. Talk to him, Ellie. It's the only way."

NIGHT HAD FALLEN by the time they'd finished eating and catching up in Reese and Sam's home above her office. Jake decided he was glad he'd come to Hay Camp, having seen for himself that Sam was doing so well. He'd spent the evening watching Ellie from the corner of his eye. A change had come over her, sitting here with her sister. That fish-out-of-water look she'd had was fading away. And for the first time, he saw what she might be like in her own world. She was something. And he wasn't sure how any woman of this time would ever live up to her. The crazy thing was, before Ellie, the idea of ever settling down with a woman had never been more than a passing thought.

So, when she had started talking about the camera at dinner, about how she'd figured out its secrets, he'd excused himself and gone outside for a smoke.

She found him standing on the second-floor porch that overlooked the street.

The stars were a smattering of pinpricks against the dome of black, which, just beyond the town's borders, seemed to be cradled by the peaks of the Black Hills. Jake crushed the last of his cheroot under his heel as she walked up behind him. She wrapped her arms around him and pressed her cheek against his back. Jake touched her hand, then turned around to fill his arms with her.

"Do you know the odds of me finding my sister were

about the same as you and me picking out the same star in that sky up there?" she said. "Thank you."

"Happy?"

"And lucky," she answered.

He let her go, turned back to the rail and leaned against it with both elbows.

"We haven't had much of a chance to talk these past few days," she said, joining him there. "With the stage-coach and…everything."

"Ellie—" he began.

"No, wait. I want to say something. I know you came here for me. This wasn't in your plan. You could've left me at any point, but you didn't. I'm grateful to you."

"Grateful." He couldn't take his eyes off the ring on her hand glittering in the dark, catching the moonlight.

"Maybe that's a bad choice of words."

"No, that sounds about right." He squeezed two fingers against the bridge of his nose, against the ache rising between his eyes.

"What's that supposed to mean?"

He straightened. "It just means I'm glad you found your sister. And whether it was meant to be or not, I'm glad I was along for the ride. We had a good time, give or take a few bumps in the road. Like you said in the beginning. It was fun. Now, I reckon, you're figurin' on using that camera to go back. 'Cause it's your rightful place and your sister's fine here. And it's none of my business, but I only have one thing to say about that, Ellie. I've been a gambling man all my life, but the idea of you trustin' yours to that thing-a-ma-jig, well, it's a bad gamble. I don't like it."

"You don't?"

"No. You think you know how it works, but what if you're wrong? What then?"

As if his words had suddenly galvanized something inside her, she asked, "What if I'm right?"

He stared at her for a moment and said, "Well, then, you'll have that, won't you?"

"Then give me a reason to stay." She'd given him a bald challenge.

"What?"

"One reason beyond my sister, who's in love and totally content with her life here. What else should keep me here, Jake, when you go?"

He lowered his head, unsure what to say. He couldn't deny it.

"You *are* going, aren't you? That's what this is about? This whole pulling-away thing? Since the boat? Leave me before I can leave you? Oh, I've been there before. I'm quite familiar with the preemptive strike. In modern psychological terms, I believe the saying goes, 'To avoid being the dump-ee, become the dump-er.'"

He frowned, not sure he followed.

"So give me one reason and I won't go."

"You're asking *me* to be the reason? That's about the most foolhardy thing that's ever come out of your mouth."

"Is it? Imagine what you'd say if I said I was in love with you."

He flinched as if she'd struck him. He didn't like this argument. Didn't like her taunting him this way. He was right and she was wrong and there was no middle ground here. "But you won't. Because if you did, you'd be saying it to a no-account—"

"I love you."

"—gambler who lives on riverboats, running from the goddamn stupid mistakes of his—"

"Did you hear me?"

"—past and that's no life for a…woman like you." He fell silent. Wishing he'd never started this.

"I've run a long way, too," she said. "All the way here. So tell me why I should stay."

He ran a hand over the bristle on his jaw. "Stay because of you, Ellie. Not because of me. Stay because it's where fate's brought you. Stay because somehow you'll find a way to take beautiful pictures of this place and people will remember you. And you'll build yourself a life with someone who deserves you. Someone who won't be looking over his shoulder for the rest of his life. Don't stay because of me."

Ellie swiped at the moisture on her cheek and got that angry look in her gray eyes. "Don't presume to tell me how to be as you're walking out the door, Jake. I'm a modern woman. I will choose for myself. And you? You will be too far away for it to matter."

She turned on her heel to go, but he grabbed her arm and pulled her hard up against him because he didn't know what else to do. He wasn't finished being angry with her for her mule-headedness, or for making him give a damn about what happened to her. She would always be able to outtalk him, outargue him because she was like a goddamn Philadelphia lawyer when she was up on her high horse. So he did the only thing he could think of. He kissed her—hard on her mouth—until she stopped pushing at him and he felt her soften in his arms. And as he kissed her, he memorized the taste of her and the way her mouth fit against his. And the soft brush of her tongue against his lips. And it nearly broke him.

Finally, he let her go and she stared up at him, her expression confused, her lips bruised with his kiss. She pressed the back of her hand to them.

And then, knowing that had been exactly the wrong thing to do, he pulled his gaze from her and stared at the floor, not finding another safe place to look.

"Wow," she said, with a weak, watery laugh. "I've been on the receiving end of a lot of goodbyes in my time, but *that*...wow, that was a good one. And the best part? You didn't even have to pony up the words. Way to go, Jake. Thanks for everything."

She turned and walked into the house and left him standing on the porch alone.

And when he walked to the Lucky Strike and ordered up a row of whiskeys at the saloon downstairs, he drank them one by one and cursed the same fate that had brought her here and that now taunted him with the possibility of happiness.

14

THREE DAYS PASSED. Then four. No sign of Jake.

She knew he'd left town. There was nothing for it. He'd gone and she would simply have to decide now what to do. Go or stay. Stay or go.

Ellie grabbed the lead rope on a gray gelding at Sam's paddock and led him into the shade to wait his turn with the farrier. The sharp smell of the smith's fire stung her nostrils every now and then as the breeze carried it to her. The blacksmith and Sam were working on shoes for another horse, and Ellie was ostensibly helping. In reality, Sam had taken pity on her and given her a job.

She picked up a brush and curried the gray horse, swiping off trail dust and speckles of mud from his legs. It was simply a task to occupy her mind. Unfortunately, her mind was racing with thoughts.

Thoughts of what faced her if she went back: Dane, and unfinished business. Her parents—who by now had no doubt given up hope of seeing either of their daughters again. Not that they ever saw much of them when they'd lived in their world. The press, explaining where she'd been.

Her friends. Her camera. Convenience.

Money.

If she left, the real cost would be this: she'd never see her sister again. Her only real family. But already she could see Reese worrying about her. Since Jake had left, she'd thought of ways to keep her occupied.

Ellie had gone on rounds with her, even helped deliver a baby late one night—the most wonderful thing she'd ever witnessed. She'd held the child wrapped in a soft cotton sheet as the mother slept. It lay small and warm in her arms, cooing the first sounds of life. She wished she had a camera then, to photograph that child. And the moment. Jake had been right about one thing at least. She had to find her passion again. A passion apart from him.

Sometimes, like now, she'd walk down to the livery to help Sam with the horses. There was something calming about the soft nuzzle of a horse's velvety nose and the alfalfa-scented breath whuffling in one's ear that was distracting. Anything, really, to keep her from thinking about Jake.

She'd rewritten her exit line a thousand times, each one seeming less what she should have said than the last. And really, what was there to say?

Forgetting Jake was equally impossible. Because he was everywhere: in the earthy scent in the white-ruffled waters of Rapid Creek; at night when she looked up at the stars; in her dreams—always in her dreams.

Maybe she should go back. Press the button and go. At least then Reese would not have to worry about her. This place and its memories would be replaced by the bustling world of the twenty-first century. Maybe she'd even begin to forget him.

"You'll spoil them," Sam said with an indulgent smile, interrupting her thoughts. "Petting them that way. Feeding them apples and sugar cubes."

Ellie let go of the gelding's muzzle guiltily. "I'm sorry. I can't help it. They're all so…cute."

The gelding nudged her in the shoulder, wanting more.

"Don't let my customers hear you saying that. Then again, maybe I should hire you permanently. The horses seem to like having you around."

She rubbed the gelding's velvety nose one more time. "I guess none of us is immune to a little love now and then, right, boy?"

Sam grinned. "Truer words were never spoken. Puddle, there's my own personal ride. Fella I bought him off had almost ruined him. Came covered with whiplashes and skittish as a jaybird. A real lunatic. Took almost six months to get a saddle on him. Now, he'll eat sugar out of your hand like a pup."

"So *you* spoiled him, then."

"I guess the orneriest ones need the gentlest hand."

Ellie smiled. Sometimes that worked and sometimes it didn't. "I'm thinking of going back, Sam."

"Back? Back where?"

"Where I belong."

His expression clouded. "You belong here, with your sister."

"No, you two have a life here."

"And you're a part of it now," he said flatly. "I'm with Jake on this. No telling what could happen with that camera."

"We've both done it once, Reese and I. We came out of it all right. It's probably no more dangerous than... riding Puddle here."

"Don't let Reese hear you talk that way. She wants you to stay. *I* want you to stay."

Ellie touched his arm. "You're a good man, Sam. Have I mentioned that I'm glad you're my brother-in-law?"

Sam shifted uncomfortably. "I better get back to these horses. There's more apples in the bin in the tack room. I reckon it can't hurt to give all of them a little something extra." He smiled at Ellie, then turned back to his work.

No, it wouldn't hurt, she decided. It wouldn't hurt at all.

JAKE HAD NOT LEFT Hay Camp. In fact, he'd barely left the tables at the Nugget beside the Lucky Strike Hotel where he'd only occasionally gone to sleep off the hangover from the night before. But the past two nights, tired of the game, he'd left the tables to wander down the always-rowdy streets filled with eager would-be miners on their way up to the fields in Deadwood Gulch. Regular gunfights erupted in the street as tempers flared and desperation got washed down with alcohol.

But late at night, he ended up at the far end of town, outside of Sam and Reese's place, watching from across the street to catch a glimpse of Ellie.

He should have left days ago. He knew that. But he stayed for reasons he couldn't quite explain. Nights, he'd spot her silhouette in the window, or see her staring up at the night sky. A hundred times he warned himself to go and let her be. And he would.

This wasn't like him. By now, he should be a hundred miles away, floating down the Missouri and taking some piker for all he had. He'd actually considered going to Deadwood, but he didn't have the stomach for it. No, he belonged on the river and that's where he'd go. Tomorrow.

He earned enough at the tables that he could buy anything he needed here to replace his kit, buy a horse and saddle, take his time. He'd ride back through Indian territory along the Cheyenne River—a smaller target on horseback than on a stage—and take his chances. If he came up lucky, then he'd consider himself ahead because that's how he figured his life. In pluses and minuses. Ellie had been a plus. A temporary one. Now he figured he was drawing even.

He took a table in a crowded smoke-filled café down the street from the Nugget and ordered milk and a steak. He hadn't eaten well in days and the alcohol was beginning to prey on his nerves without some food in his belly. The restaurant stayed open late hours to support the staggering numbers of men passing through Hay Camp on their way to the goldfields.

The hastily built raw wood tables around him were full of men. Only a handful of women ever made it this far west. Except, of course, Reese and Ellie, and those fancy girls who worked the other side of the table. There were plenty of them imported from the East where immigrants found life in America harder than they'd imagined.

When his food arrived, the waiter set it down in front of him. "That how you like it?" he asked.

"It's fine," Jake answered, cutting into the pink center of the steak.

"Thank God," the waiter mumbled.

"Beg pardon?"

"Nothin'. Just that I couldn't hardly stomach servin' another bloody one."

It only took a heartbeat for that to register. Jake grabbed the man's arm as he walked away. "What did you say?"

"Hey, now—!"

Jake let him go. "What did you just say?"

The pie-faced waiter shook his sleeve straight and scowled at Jake. "I don't want no trouble."

"About the steak. The raw steak."

"What about it?"

"Who ordered it?"

"Tallish, gray-haired feller. Pale-blue eyes. Ate that whole steak nearly raw. Ain't never seen nothin' like it. Says to me when he orders, 'Let it kiss the griddle once on each side and if it ain't still bleeding when I get it, then—'"

Jake pulled his pistol from the back of his waistband. "How long ago was that? Did you see where he went?"

The waiter eyed the gun warily. "Left twenty minutes 'fore you come in. And can't say I watched where he went. Somethin' about that fella made my neck hair rise."

Jake reached in his pocket for three bits and tossed it on the table.

"Hey, what about your steak?"

"Was he alone?" Jake asked him.

"Yessir. I reckon maybe he was fixin' to head up to the goldfields though."

"Why do you say that?"

"Because like every other piker comes into town on the stage, he wanted to know where Keegan's Livery was."

BY THE TIME Jake got to Sam's, a cold sweat was pouring down his face and he had forgotten to breathe for the last block. And when he did, he smelled smoke.

He caught a glimpse of a shadowy figure rushing from Reese's downstairs office into the alleyway, disappearing into the darkness. Jake raised his pistol and started to follow, but caught the flicker of an unnatural light in the window of the office and the crackling sound of a fire.

Racing closer, he spotted flames already licking at the ceiling, and one of the windows exploded from the heat.

No.

He ran into the office, past the wall of smoke. The fire flickered brightly. Brightly enough to see Sam lying on the floor of the office, his gun still in his hand. Reese was bent over him, trying to pull him out.

Jake reached for him and grabbed him by the coat.

"Jake! Thank God—" Reese cried, coughing, her mouth and nose ringed with soot. "Help me get Sam out! That man knocked the lamp over fighting with him!"

Together they pulled as Sam swam back to consciousness and the fire exploded to life behind them. Reese's entire office went up then the flames licked their way up the stairwell toward the rooms upstairs.

"Where's Ellie?" Jake shouted.

"She's still up there! Oh, Jake, please, we have to get her! Sam heard a noise downstairs and I followed him—"

Sam coughed and rolled to his side, spitting out blood. "Son of a bitch…was looking for the camera, and Ellie, she's in the back room—"

Jake bolted toward the second-story porch and pulled himself up the post underneath it. He reached for the railing that ran across the porch, yelling for Ellie.

Miraculously, she appeared at the edge of the smoke like an apparition. She was coughing, her nightdress stained with soot. She was holding her camera.

As he pulled himself up to the railing, the sound of a gunshot came from behind him, accompanied by a fiery kick of heat that stabbed through his upper arm. The blow knocked him sideways. He lost his grip and fell eight feet back to the hard-packed earth.

The fall stole his breath. Above him, he could hear the crackle of the fire and, dimly, the sound of Ellie, screaming his name.

Jake blindly grabbed for the gun tucked into his belt with his left hand, but he heard another sound, this one closer to his ear. The sound of a gun cocking.

He didn't have time to look up. Besson yanked him up by the collar, wrapped an arm around his neck and pressed the gun to his temple.

Jake wanted to kill him. Twice caught by this son of a bitch was two times too many. He watched Ellie, backlit by the fire. She was standing at the edge of the balcony, tears streaming down her sooty face.

"Jake, do what he says. It's this camera he wants, not you!"

Besson loosened his grip on Jake's neck so he could put the gun down.

"You," Besson yelled at Reese, "get over here!"

But Sam pulled her to him.

"You leave her out of this, you son of a bitch."

"Ever the hero, eh, Sam?"

"Your death is long overdue," Sam answered. "I'm going to kill you and I'm gonna—"

"Sam!" Reese shouted in fear. "Please do what he says."

Besson hollered, "For now, Sam, you're just going to catch the camera she's going to drop down to you, real nice and easy. 'Cause if you drop it, I'll kill him," he said, shoving the gun harder against Jake's temple, "and then I'll kill your little woman."

Smoke was pouring out behind Ellie. It was only a matter of minutes before the whole place gave way.

Jake had a hand clapped against his upper arm, but blood was leaking past his fingers. He'd handled this whole thing all wrong. Telling her to stay. Besson meant to finish him and Sam regardless of what she did. Even from this distance the heat from the fire was growing intense. There was only one thing he could do for Ellie now.

"Push the button, Ellie! Push it and go back. He'll never find you. It'll be all right. Just go!"

Ellie stared at him in horror.

"Shut up!" Besson growled, pressing the gun's barrel harder against his temple. "Shut the hell up!"

"Push it now, Ellie. Do it!"

But Ellie shook her head, holding the camera poised at the balcony's edge. Flames licked the wooden floor behind her now and roared out the window. Up the street, he could hear the panicked shouts of "Fire!" as the flames climbed high above the rooftops.

"Ellie, for God's sake! Push the button!"

Ellie shook her head and told Besson, "Here, you want this camera so bad? Then you'd better catch it!" And she heaved the camera in a high, sweeping arc over the head of Besson.

"Nooo!" he screamed, dropping Jake and running for the camera, which was already plummeting to the street. Besson dove to catch it, but it hit the ground with a satisfying explosion of wood and glass. Shards flew everywhere. Besson roared in fury.

Jake grabbed for his gun and turned with it just as Besson swung his pistol toward Ellie.

Jake squeezed the trigger, felt the gun kick in his hand. Besson stumbled backward with a look of surprise on his face and a blossom of red sprouting on his chest. He landed flat on his back in the dirt, clawed there with his heels, then never moved again.

When Jake turned to Ellie, she was already climbing over the balcony to Sam, who was holding his arms out for her. The fire was a scorching wave of heat.

"Jump, Ellie!" Sam cried.

She did, right into his arms as the brigade of men with fire buckets came running up the street. Sam ran away from the fire, then set her down. Reese was there, colliding with her in a fierce hug.

"Oh, El! That was insane, you know that, right?" Reese held her tight, tears running down her cheeks. "I was so scared for you…for all of us. Thank you."

"Your place! I'm so sorry!" Ellie cried. "Look at it."

The roof caved in then, sending a storm of sparks and flame shooting in the air.

Reese shook her head. "It's just wood. Just pieces of wood and a few medical supplies. We can replace it. All of it." She glanced at Jake, who was covering his wound and moving toward the broken camera. "There's some things you can never replace. Ever."

Jake bent down and picked up the pieces of the camera. Ellie squeezed Reese in a hug, then moved beside him.

"Jake?"

He looked up, as near tears as she'd ever seen him. He was holding the broken shards in his hands.

"Your arm—"

"It's just a furrow. It'll be fine." He dropped his gaze down to the mess he held. "But maybe we can fix it."

"Fix what?"

"The camera. Maybe we can find a way to—"

"I don't give a damn about the camera," she said. "Come here."

He stood up, dropping the pieces.

"Right here," she said, wiggling her opened arms.

He slipped between them, dragged her up against him and laid a kiss on her that carried with it all the desperation and regret she knew he must be feeling. They both tasted of smoke. Ellie curled her fingers into his hair, pulling him closer, pressing her breasts to his chest. When she broke the kiss, it was because she had something more to say.

"Wait. You mean to tell me you've been here all along and you let me think you'd gone?" she demanded.

He gave a sheepish grin. "Yep."

"Well, that was just wrong, Mr. Gannon."

"Right. I mean, that's true."

She twisted the hair at the back of his neck around her fingers. "And do you have anything to say in your defense?"

"Just one thing." He leaned closer and whispered it in her ear.

She blinked hard. "I'm sorry. Did…did you just say I love you?"

His grin turned slightly wicked then. "Yep."

Ellie shook her head. "I'm sorry, could you just say that loud enough for the others to hear because frankly I don't think they'll believe me when I tell them that—"

He shut her up with a slow, deep kiss, holding her tight with his good arm as she clung to his neck. When they came up for air, her eyes were brimming with tears.

"I don't know why it took me so long to admit it," he told her, dragging a thumb across the soot on her cheek. "I'm sorry I—"

"Shh," she hushed. "Do you remember when you told me if you were a camera you'd see that I was a woman who'd never been touched enough? You were right about that. I was just waiting for the right man to do the touching, I guess. But I never told you what I'd see if I was a camera looking at you. I can now. And I should've said it to you on the porch that night before you left."

He watched her, waiting.

"I'd see—" she dragged a finger across his lips and smiled "—my future."

Jake took her fingertip into his mouth and kissed it.

"Hard to say what that's gonna hold, Ellie. But I can't seem to see mine without you in it, either. So better make that *our* future," he said, then glanced at the commotion behind them. "Just as soon as we help Sam and your sister rebuild theirs. Turns out I did pretty well at the tables these past few days. Maybe even have enough to start my own casino here. Get on the other side of the tables."

It was like him, Ellie thought, to think of Sam and Reese first. It's what she loved about him. And it was there all the time, even when he didn't believe it himself. "Jake, that's brilliant."

"Yeah, but what about you? Aren't you gonna miss all those things back there? Those…whatdya call them…airplanes and plastic buying cards and…and your money?"

She would miss the airplanes. And the computer and maybe the makeup, but tonight had cleared up much of that in her head. It had set her priorities straight. And she knew exactly what she wanted. "Well," she said, "we have your expertise at the poker tables, I can find my way around a camera…and there's the ring. And, well, I might just know a little something about the future…"

He smiled. "Maybe you should set up a fortune-teller's tent."

"Maybe I should. Maybe I could tell your fortune?"

"Yeah?"

"I predict that you're gonna kiss me right now. And for the next fifty or sixty years. On a regular basis."

"Pretty sure of yourself."

"Mmm-hmm."

"You are good, Visa. You're very, very good." And he kissed her indeed, soundly and well.

And it was just as it should have been.

* * * * *

Don't miss
ONCE A REBEL,
the next novel in the
STOLEN FROM TIME *miniseries.*
Available from Harlequin Blaze
May 2009!

*Celebrate 60 years of pure
reading pleasure with Harlequin®!*

*Step back in time and enjoy a
sneak preview of an exciting anthology
from Harlequin® Historical with*
THE DIAMONDS OF WELBOURNE MANOR.

This compelling anthology features three stories
about the outrageous Fitzmanning sisters. Meet
Annalise, who is never at a loss for words… But
that can change with an unexpected encounter in
the forest.

*Available May 2009
from Harlequin® Historical.*

"I'm the illegitimate daughter of notoriously scandalous parents, Mr. Milford. Candidates for my hand are unlikely to be lining up at the gates."

"Don't be so quick to discount your charms, my dear. Or the charm of your substantial dowry. Or even your brothers' influence. There are as many reasons to marry as there are marriages."

Annalise snorted. "Oh, yes. Perhaps I shall marry for dynastic reasons, or perhaps for property or influence. After all, a loveless, practical marriage worked out so well for my mother."

"Well, you've routed me on that one. I can think of no suitable rejoinder." Ned rose to his feet and extended his hand. "And since that is the case, let me be the first to wish you a long and happy spinsterhood."

Her mouth gaped open. And then she laughed.

And he froze.

This was the first time, Ned realized. The first time he'd seen her eyes light up and her mouth curl. The first time he'd witnessed her features melded together in glorious accord to produce exquisite beauty.

Unbelievable what a change came over her face. Unheard-of what effect her throaty, rasping laughter had on his body. It pounded a beat upon his ear, quickly taken up by his pulse. It echoed through him, finally residing in his stirring nether regions.

So easily she did it, awakened these sensations within him—without any apparent effort at all. And she had called him potentially dangerous? Clearly the intelligent thing for him to do would be to steer clear, to leave her to the tender ministrations of Lord Peter Blackthorne.

"You were right." She smiled up at him as she took his hand and climbed to her feet. "I do feel better."

Ah, well. When had he ever chosen the intelligent path?

He did not relinquish her hand. He used it to pull her in, close enough that he could feel the warmth of her. "At the risk of repeating Lord Peter's mistake and anticipating too much—may I ask if you'll be my partner in battledore tomorrow?"

Her smiled dimmed. Her breath came a little faster. His own had gone shallow, as if he'd just run a race—and lost. He ran his gaze over the appealing lift of her brow and the curious angle of her chin. His index finger twitched.

"I should like that," she said.

His finger trembled again and he lifted it, traced the pink and tender shell of her ear, the unique sweep of her jaw. Her pulse leaped beneath her skin, triggering his own. Slowly he tilted her chin up, waiting for her to object, to step back, to slap his hand away.

She did none of those eminently sensible things. Which left him free to do the entirely impractical thing.

Baby soft, the skin of her lips. Her whole body trembled when he touched her there.

He leaned in. Her eyes closed, even as she stood straight against him, strung as tight as a bow. He pressed his mouth to hers. It was a soft kiss, sweet and chaste. And yet he was hot and hard and as ready as he'd ever been in his life.

She drew back a little. Sighed. Their breath mingled a moment before she slowly backed away.

"Oh," she breathed. Her dark eyes were full of wonder and something that looked like fear. He took a step toward her, but she only shook her head. His outstretched hand fell to his side as she turned to disappear into the wood. This was the first time, Ned realized. The first time, since he'd come to the house party at Welbourne Manor, that he'd seen her eyes light up.

* * * * *

Follow Ned and Annalise's story
in May 2009 in
THE DIAMONDS OF WELBOURNE MANOR.
Available May 2009
from Harlequin® Historical.

Available in the series romance section,
or in the historical romance section,
wherever books are sold.

We'll be spotlighting a different series
every month throughout 2009
to celebrate our 60th anniversary.

Look for Harlequin® Historical in May!

Celebrations begin with
a sumptuous Regency house party!

Join three scandalous sisters in

**THE DIAMONDS OF
WELBOURNE MANOR**

Glittering, scintillating, sensual fun
by Diane Gaston, Deb Marlowe
and Amanda McCabe.

60 years of Harlequin,
600 years of romance
in Harlequin Historical!

Harlequin® Historical
Historical Romantic Adventure!

If you enjoyed reading
Joanne Rock in the
Harlequin® Blaze™ series,
look for her new book
from Harlequin® Historical!

THE KNIGHT'S RETURN
Joanne Rock

Missing more than his memory,
Hugh de Montagne sets out to find his
true identity. When he lands in a small
Irish kingdom and finds a new liege in the
Irish king, his hands are full with his new
assignment: guarding the king's beautiful,
exiled daughter. Sorcha has had her heart
broken by a knight in the past. Will she be
able to open her heart to love again?

Available April
wherever books are sold.

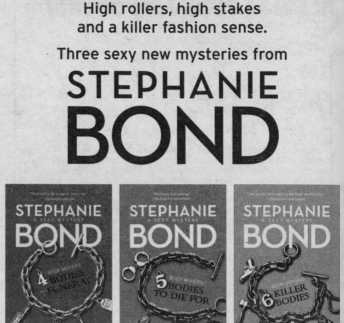

REQUEST YOUR FREE BOOKS!

2 FREE NOVELS PLUS 2 FREE GIFTS!

HARLEQUIN®

Blaze™

Red-hot reads!

YES! Please send me 2 FREE Harlequin® Blaze™ novels and my 2 FREE gifts (gifts are worth about $10). After receiving them, if I don't wish to receive any more books, I can return the shipping statement marked "cancel". If I don't cancel, I will receive 6 brand-new novels every month and be billed just $4.24 per book in the U.S. or $4.71 per book in Canada. Shipping and handling is just 25¢ per book. That's a savings of 15% or more off the cover price! I understand that accepting the 2 free books and gifts places me under no obligation to buy anything. I can always return a shipment and cancel at any time. Even if I never buy another book, the two free books and gifts are mine to keep forever.

151 HDN ERVA 351 HDN ERUX

Name _____ (PLEASE PRINT) _____

Address _____ Apt. # _____

City _____ State/Prov. _____ Zip/Postal Code _____

Signature (if under 18, a parent or guardian must sign)

Mail to the **Harlequin Reader Service:**
IN U.S.A.: P.O. Box 1867, Buffalo, NY 14240-1867
IN CANADA: P.O. Box 609, Fort Erie, Ontario L2A 5X3

Not valid to current subscribers of Harlequin Blaze books.

**Want to try two free books from another line?
Call 1-800-873-8635 or visit www.morefreebooks.com.**

HB09R

COMING NEXT MONTH

Available April 28, 2009

#465 HOT-WIRED Jennifer LaBrecque
From 0–60

Drag racer/construction company owner Beau Stillwell has his hands full trying to mess up his sister's upcoming wedding. The guy just isn't good enough for her. But when Beau meets Natalie Bridges, the very determined wedding planner, he realizes he needs to change gears and do something drastic. Like drive sexy, uptight Natalie absolutely wild...

#466 LET IT RIDE Jillian Burns

What better place for grounded flyboy Cole Jackson to blow off some sexual steam than Vegas, baby! Will his campaign to seduce casino beauty Jordan Brenner crash and burn, once she discovers what he really wants to bet?

#467 ONCE A REBEL Debbi Rawlins
Stolen from Time, Bk. 3

Maggie Dawson is stunned when the handsomest male *ever* appears from the future, insisting on her help! Cord Braddock's out of step in the 1870s Wild West, although courting sweet, sexy Maggie comes as naturally to him as the sun rising over the Dakota hills....

#468 GOING DOWN HARD Tawny Weber

When Sierra Donovan starts receiving indecent pictures of herself—with threats attached—she knows she's going to need help. But the last person she needs it from is sexy security expert Reece Carter. Although, if Sierra's back has to be against the wall, she can't think of anyone she'd rather put her there....

#469 AFTERBURN Kira Sinclair
Uniformly Hot!

Air force captain Chase Carden knows life will be different now that he's back from Iraq—he's already been told he'll be leading the Thunderbird Squadron. Little does he guess that his biggest change will come in the person of Rina McAllister, his last one-night stand...who's now claiming to be his wife!

#470 MY SEXY GREEK SUMMER Marie Donovan

A wicked vacation is what Cara Sokol has promised herself, although she has to keep her identity a secret! Hottie Yannis Petridis is exactly what she's looking for *and* he's good with secrets—he's got one of his own!

www.eHarlequin.com